", you've brought in a hired gun to help you hang onto your property."

"You want my ranch bad?" Calamity asked, facing the woman.

"I intend to have it!"

"All right, then. I'll go get the deeds from the law-wrangler right now. Then you 'n' me'll go round to the Wells Fargo corral. Just us. Not my 'hired gun'—nor you'rn. And you can have them deeds . . . If you can take 'em offen me."

A small crowd had gathered, taking in every word. Calamity's suggestion brought a muted rumble of comment from the audience. Clenching her fists, the blonde studied Calamity with hate-filled eyes. Then, slowly, Florence let her hands drop to her sides.

"I'm a businesswoman, not some cat-house tail-peddler," the blonde sniffed. "I'll give you—"

"I've told you the price for my ranch," Calamity cut in flatly. "That you—just you—take it off me."

Florence glared with rage and determination.

"You've had my last offer," she said. "And this county's not big enough to hold me and anybody who's against me."

Books by J.T. Edson

RANCH WAR
THE BIG HUNT
THE ROAD TO RATCHET CREEK
RUNNING IRONS
WACO'S BADGE
TEXAS KILLERS
COLD DECK, HOT LEAD

J.T. EDSON

RANCH WAR

HarperTorch
An Imprint of HarperCollinsPublishers

◆

HARPERTORCH
An Imprint of HarperCollins*Publishers*
10 East 53rd Street
New York, New York 10022-5299

Copyright © 1970 by J. T. Edson
Originally published in the UK as *White Stallion, Red Mare*
ISBN-13: 978-0-06-078424-9
ISBN-10: 0-06-078424-5

First HarperTorch paperback printing: June 2006

HarperCollins®, HarperTorch™, and ◆ ™ are trademarks of HarperCollins Publishers Inc.

Printed in the United States of America

Visit HarperTorch on the World Wide Web at www.harpercollins.com

10 9 8 7 6 5 4 3 2 1

RANCH
WAR

Chapter 1

AIN'T YOU CALAMITY JANE?

THE NIGHT CLERK OF THE SELECT, EXPENSIVE RAILroad House Hotel stared with disapproval at the prospective client approaching his reception desk. Despite the law-abiding conditions which made Mulrooney almost unique among the Kansas railroad and trail-end towns,* unescorted females rarely made an appearance in search of a room. Still less when the time had gone ten o'clock. And the few who did come belonged to the best class of visitor. Herbert L. Philpotter studied the girl and decided that she had definitely come to the wrong establishment if she wanted accommodation for the night.

---

* The reasons for Mulrooney's law-abiding conditions are told in *The Trouble Busters* and *The Making of a Lawman*.

Five foot seven in height, the girl had a pretty, tanned, slightly freckled face that expressed a cheery zest for living and disregard for the conventions. Perched at a jaunty angle on her mop of shortish, curly red hair was a battered U.S. Cavalry kepi. That and her fringed buckskin jacket were not too far beyond the social pale, if not generally worn by ladies. What lay under the jacket, exposed by its open front, caused Philpotter serious misgivings. She had on a man's tartan shirt, open at the neck and down to one button lower than might be deemed decorous, especially when the garment in question appeared either to have been bought a size too small, or to have shrunk after washing. It emphasized the rich, full swell of her bosom and slender waist in a way that hinted she wore little beneath it. Inside the tightly stretched material of her Levi's pants, well-formed buttocks and hips curved down attractively to hint at the shapely quality of her legs. Her low-heeled, calf-high boots were sturdy, practical, but unfeminine.

Instead of the small grip with which most female guests arrived, the girl carried a fair-sized *parfleche* bag of buffalo hide in her left hand. The parasol much favored by ladies of fashion was replaced in her right fist by a Winchester Model 1866 carbine. Nor did her armament end there. Around her waist, slanting down to the right thigh, was a gunbelt. An ivory-handled Colt Navy revolver hung butt forward in a carefully designed holster at the right of the belt and the handle of a coiled, long-lashed bull whip was thrust into a loop at the left.

"Howdy," the girl greeted, setting down her bag and placing the carbine by the open register on the desk's top. "Do you have a room for me?"

"I—Er—That is——" Philpotter spluttered, wondering how to frame a refusal which would not provoke a rowdy protest from its recipient.

"Either you have, or you ain't," the girl stated cheerfully. "Only I was told to come here. The name's Canary. Martha Jane Canary."

"Can——" Philpotter started to repeat the name. "*You* are Miss Canary?"

"If I'm not, somebody sure played a dirty trick on my mammy," the girl replied, then went on, thinking of her last meeting with her mother,* "and on me, comes to that. Thing being, that fancy law-wrangler, Grosvenor, back to Topeka told me's there'd be a room waiting here for me."

"Oh yes, Miss—Canary," Philpotter gulped. There had been a telegraph message from the prominent Topeka lawyer asking that she be accommodated. "We have a room reserved for you."

"Now *that's* a relief." Miss Canary smiled, guessing at the cause of the prissy, chubby clerk's perturbation. The Railroad House was not her usual kind of accommodation. "Happen I'd found out he was joshing me, I'd've headed back to the

---

* Told in the "Better than Calamity" episode of *The Wildcats*.

big city 'n' asked him real polite-like why he'd done it."

"There won't be any need for that, I'm sure," Philpotter replied hurriedly, turning the open book around and indicating a pen. "If you'll fill in the register, Miss Canary, I'll have you shown to your room." He raised his voice, "Boy!"

Usually the bell-hop would have required more than one shout before making an appearance. Not that night. He came scuttling from where he had been peering through the door leading to the rear section of the ground floor. Dressed in a brass-buttoned suit and pill-box hat no less jauntily angled than Miss Canary's kepi, he displayed none of the clerk's concern over her style of clothing. Ogling her from head to toe with frank interest and approbation, he skidded to a halt at the desk.

"Take Miss Canary's bag and—firearm—to Room Fourteen," Philpotter ordered, placing a key by the carbine. "You don't mind being at the rear, Miss Canary?"

"Front or back's all one to me, 's long's I get a bed," the girl answered.

Bending to pick up the girl's *parfleche,* the bell-hop lowered his eyes along the front of her shirt. His gaze halted at the gunbelt, taking in the bullwhip it supported. Jolting erect as if stung by a bee, he stared at her with increased admiration.

"Ain't you Calamity Jane?" the boy gasped.

"I'd have to say 'yes' to that," Miss Canary admitted.

Shock twisted at Philpotter's pompous features and he gobbled, "Bu-Bu-But you said——"

"That I'm Martha Jane Canary," grinned the girl. "I am. Hell, mister, you don't reckon that the preacher said, 'I christen this-here beautiful lil gal who's wetting all down the front of my best shirt Calamity Jane.' Now do you?"

"Er—No!" Philpotter answered, popping out the word like the cork from a champagne bottle. "I suppose not."

"And 'Martha's' one helluva name to tie on to a sweet-looking, lovable lil gal like me, ain't it?"

"Er—Yes, I suppose it is," the clerk croaked. Wanting time to think out the latest development, he continued, "But why do they call you *Calamity* Jane?"

"Now that's something I've never figured out myself," the girl replied, raising her eyes piously to the roof. "There's not a more loving-natured, better-tempered gal from here to there and back the long way. I sure don't know why folks call me 'Calamity.' "

Which was far from being the truth. In fact, Miss Martha Jane Canary might honestly claim that she had earned the sobriquet on a number of occasions. Not because she was clumsy, incompetent or accident-prone. It was just that trouble came her way like a homing-pigeon finding its loft.

Early in her life, Calamity's father had headed West to find a fortune. When neither he nor it returned, Charlotte Canary had left her children in the care of a St. Louis convent and gone to look for him. There had been too much of her mother's reckless spirit in Martha Jane for her to accept convent discipline. Always a tomboy, she had run away on her sixteenth birthday and hidden in a freight-wagon going West. A variety of circumstances had combined to prevent her ignominious return to the convent. By the end of the journey, Dobe Killem's drivers had accepted her as a lucky mascot and protégé. From them she had received a practical, if unorthodox education.

While a mite shy on book-learning, she knew how to handle, care for and maintain a six-horse freight-wagon. She also possessed a reasonable ability in the use of firearms and knew how to live when on the rolling plains of the West. In her hands, the long-lashed bull-whip became a means of inducement for recalcitrant horses; or a deadly weapon. Specially plaited for her by Dobe Killem, the whip had a slightly more slender, but no shorter lash than those used by his male drivers. She was very expert in its use.

The nickname had come into being through her penchant for becoming involved in a variety of trouble. Going into saloons with the other drivers had often brought her into conflict with the female employees. Jealous of her intrusion, more than one saloon girl had tried to evict Calamity. Leading a more healthy life than her opponents, Calamity had only once—during her last meeting with Charlotte Canary—met defeat at another woman's hands. She had been held to a draw when she tangled with Belle Starr in Elkhorn, Montana, after which she had smuggled the lady outlaw out of town in her wagon to avoid Belle's arrest by the local marshal.*

Not all the excitement that followed Calamity came from saloon brawls. She had taken her full share of fighting off Indians and other marauders with designs on the wagons' cargoes. Along with Belle Starr and Belle Boyd, the Rebel Spy,† she had been responsible for breaking up a murderous outlaw gang.‡ After its driver had been wounded in an Indian attack, she had driven a stagecoach to its destination, then helped a U.S. Marshal to trap a smart owlhoot.§ The citizens of New Orleans had had cause to be grateful for Calamity's visit. While there, she had battled with a *savate*-fighting Creole girl, embroiling her friends in a rough-house that wrecked a saloon; but she had also acted as a decoy against a maniacal murderer who had strangled

---

* Told in the "The Bounty On Belle Starr's Scalp" episode of *Troubled Range*.

† Belle Boyd's story is told in *The Colt and the Sabre, The Rebel Spy, The Bloody Border* and *The Hooded Riders*.

‡ Told in *The Bad Bunch*.

§ Told in *Calamity Spells Trouble*.

eight women in the city's parks, ending his reign of terror.* More recently, she had sided a Texas Ranger in ending the activities of a band of cow thieves.†

So while she deserved the name "Calamity"—and knew it—most of her escapades had been on the side of law and order.

Studying the girl, who looked so sincere that she might have been telling the truth, Philpotter decided against taking the matter of her pseudonym further. There was another item troubling him. While he had heard of Calamity Jane, there had never been any mention of her as Martha Jane Canary. He wondered how he could raise the subject of proving her identity without creating a scene, or giving offense to somebody who might have influential connections.

"Have you eaten, Miss Canary?" he asked, for something to say.

"Ate right well on the train," Calamity replied. "Ole Freddie Woods sure travels in style."

"*You* know Miss Woods?" Philpotter gulped.

"Sure," Calamity agreed.

Having gauged the clerk's character and guessed what was on his mind, she figured he would be easier to get along with if he knew that she was one of Freddie Woods' friends. In addition to being the co-owner of Mulrooney's best saloon, Freddie was

---

* Told in *The Bull Whip Breed*.

† Told in *The Cow Thieves*.

the town's efficient mayor. The assumption paid off. Giving a cough, Philpotter signaled to the boy to take Calamity upstairs.

Lifting the *parfleche,* the boy grunted a little as he became aware of its weight. His opinion of Calamity Jane had shot up several notches. In addition to the way she handled old "Potty," which he could admire knowing the man, she had toted the heavy bag all the way from the railroad depot. Picking up her carbine, Calamity followed the boy across the hall.

Philpotter shook his head as he watched them go. One had to remember that Miss Woods tended to be unconventional and made unusual friends. So he did not intend to antagonize Miss Canary. Anyway, he consoled himself, the room was only reserved for one night. With luck, its occupant would have taken her departure in the morning before the other guests left their rooms. Giving a sigh, he looked at the register. Noticing that the girl had not signed it, he completed the appropriate columns. "Miss M. J. Canary, Topeka. Room Fourteen."

"You couldn't've surprised old Potty any more if you'd hit him in the face with a sock-full of bull-droppings, Calamity," the boy enthused as they mounted the stairs. "Did you really eat with Miss Freddie on the train?"

"Sure I did," Calamity replied. "And shared a couple of bottles of what she called wine. I tell you, it'll never replace whiskey for drinking."

"Where-at's your wagon?"

"With Dobe Killem's freight outfit. Ought to be here in a week or so."

"Air it true that your team can run faster'n pronghorn antelope?"

"Not when they're hauling a full load," Calamity admitted modestly. "Any trail crews in town?"

"A couple. Panhandle outfits," the youngster replied. "It's early yet. Must be, the OD Connected ain't arrived."

By that time they had reached the door of Room Fourteen. Unlocking and opening it, the boy stood aside and let her enter.

"Will it do?" he asked, when he had lit the lamp.

Coming to a halt, Calamity looked around her. The lamp hanging in the center of the ceiling illuminated far more elegant quarters than she usually occupied. On the left of the door was a double bed with a mattress of considerable thickness and clean white sheets. The other furnishings comprised of a wardrobe with a full-length mirror fitted to its door, a dressing-table, two chairs and a washstand holding a jug, soap and a white towel bearing the hotel's name. Heavy drapes were closed across the window opposite the door.

"Whoee!" Calamity breathed, completing her examination. "Won't it, though."

Placing her *parfleche* on the bed, the boy received a tip and left. Calamity rested her carbine against the bed's top right-side post. Removing her jacket, she crossed to the wardrobe and hung it inside. Returning to the bed, she took off her gunbelt and hung it over the post above the carbine. Then she tested the mattress for comfort by bouncing her rump up and down on it a couple of times.

"Whee doggie!" Calamity breathed, standing up. "Ain't this a pistol? I don't know why the law-wrangler here in town wants to see me, but him and that Governor sure know how to treat a gal. Which I surely do deserve all this comfort."

While peeling off her shirt, she sniffed the air. Whoever had occupied the room previously used a strong, sickly perfume that was not to her taste. However, something else took her mind off the scent.

"Danged wine!" she muttered and looked under the bed. Going to its left side, she bent and drew out the chamber-pot. It was in keeping with the general elegance of the room. "Ole Chan Sing serves up our chow in a dish that's not this fancy."

With that thought, she made use of the pot and returned it. Stripping off her clothes, she gave thought to her present affluent situation. It had begun when a member of the Pinkerton National Detective Agency had met her in Ellsworth and requested that she should accompany him to the office of a prominent attorney-at-law in Topeka. Things being quiet in the freighting business, Dobe Killem had allowed her to take a vacation and she had traveled to the State's capitol with the Pink-eye.

Calamity chuckled as she thought of Lawyer Grosvenor's almost pop-eyed astonishment when he had first seen her. Recovering fast, he had seated her at his desk and started to ask questions.

Was she Martha Jane, oldest child of Robert Howard and Charlotte Martha Canary and had she been born in Princeton, Missouri?

On Calamity admitting that she was and had, he had asked, politely enough, if she could prove it. More by luck than good management, she had been able to do so. During a visit to St. Louis, she had called at the convent. On Dobe Killem's suggestion, the mother superior had handed over all the documents concerning Calamity that had been left by Charlotte in the sisters' care. So the girl had possessed the means to establish her identity.

Examining the papers, Grosvenor had admitted that she was indeed Martha Jane Canary; which Calamity had never doubted. Then he had requested that she should travel to Mulrooney, where Counselor Talbot would tell her something to her advantage. Having been closer to Mulrooney than to Topeka when the Pink-eye met her, Calamity had expressed her intention of telling *him* something to his advantage should they meet again. However, the lawyer had pointed but that the agent was only following orders, it having been assumed that she would be found in the East. More than that, all her expenses would be paid.

On learning that Calamity would not reach Mulrooney until around ten o'clock at night, Grosvenor had promised to telegraph and reserve a room for her at the Railroad House Hotel. She had hinted that she would be satisfied with some less opulent surroundings, but he was adamant. To make up for her inconvenience, she must be accommodated in the town's best hotel.

Never a girl to look a gift-horse in the mouth, Calamity had accepted. Meeting Freddie Woods on the train had been enjoyable. They had discussed the reason for Calamity's trip without reaching any conclusions. Not that Calamity worried. Her philosophy—although she had never heard the word—had always been to live for today and let tomorrow take care of itself.

Clad only in a pair of knee-long cotton drawers, Calamity drew open the covers. Then the aroma of the perfume crept back. Knowing that she would never sleep because of it, she crossed to the window. Drawing open the drapes a little, she discovered that no building overlooked the room. So she pulled them right back and raised the bottom half of the window a few inches. Putting out the light, she was approaching the bed when the call of nature struck again. Cursing Freddie's wine, she made further use of the chamber-pot before climbing into bed.

At first Calamity reveled in the unaccustomed sensation of sinking into a soft feather mattress, between clean sheets and using a down-filled pillow. Then she found herself unable to settle down. Used to much rougher conditions, bedding down on the unyielding floor of her wagon or in less luxurious surroundings than the Railroad House, she found its comforts a mixed blessing.

Time dragged by and the noises of the town died away as midnight passed. Calamity still tossed and turned as sleep continued to elude her. Although the building had been silent for at least an hour, a crack of light still glinted beneath her door. She guessed that the passage outside was kept illuminated all night for the benefit of guests returning late to their rooms. Wanting to blame something for her inability to sleep, she laid the fault on the slight glow under the door and developed a hatred for its source.

"Damned if I don't go out there and bust that blasted lamp!" she muttered, without any intention of doing it. "If this's what living in——"

A faint thud from outside the window brought her comments to a halt and caused her to sit up. Peering through the darkness, she could detect nothing to account for the sound. Deciding that it must have been imagination, she slumped back and turned on to her right side. Scowling across the bed, she eyed the door malevolently. Then an uneasy feeling that something was wrong began to seep through her.

After a moment's thought, she realized what was wrong. Looking again, she found that there was no longer an unbroken line of light at the base of the door. Instead, it had become split into three separate segments. Somebody was standing outside, his or her feet breaking the disturbing elongated glow. At first Calamity assumed that another of the hotel's guests had come to her door by mistake.

The assumption only lasted for an instant.

Lifting herself on to the right elbow, she watched a sheet of newspaper slide through the space between the bottom of the door and the floor. Maybe her formal education had been neglected, but she understood the full implications of what she saw. Sufficiently well for her to take instant action.

Rolling out of the bed on the side away from the door, she sank into a kneeling position by it. From there she watched the key, which the boy had brought inside and she had turned before undressing, begin to creep slowly backward from the lock. It fell with a gentle clink on to the sheet of paper. After a brief pause, while the intruder in the passage waited to hear if the room's occupant had been disturbed and meant to raise the alarm, the paper started to move at a snail's pace in the direction from which it had come.

"If you're fixing to come in here and rob poor, sleeping lil me," Calamity breathed, "you've got one helluva surprise headed your way."

Chapter 2

HE SURE WON'T SMELL LIKE A ROSE

~~~

EVEN AS THE SENTIMENT LEFT HER LIPS, CALAMITY realized that she had committed a serious error in tactics. Her Winchester carbine, with twelve flat-nosed Tyler B. Henry .44 cartridges in its magazine tube, was leaning against the head of the bed; but on the opposite side to her position. Worse than that; her gunbelt, holding the Navy Colt and coiled bull-whip, was draped around the bed-post above the carbine.

About to rise and rectify the mistake, she heard another faint sound from outside the window. Turning her head, she found that she had a better view. What she discovered was not comforting. Two square-shaped knobs appeared to have sprouted above the straight line of the windowsill. Before a somewhat larger, more oval shape started to rise between them, she had identified the protuberances as the top end of a ladder. It most certainly had not been there when she had pulled the drapes. Nor did she need closer observation to know the rising shape was the head of a man.

Taken with the disappearance of her key, riding slowly under the door on the retreating sheet of newspaper, the presence of a man ascending a ladder to her window rang a whole series of alarm bells for Calamity.

Listening for the click that would warn her the man in the passage was making use of the key, Calamity watched the shape across the room develop into a bare head and wide shoulders as the second intruder rose higher on the ladder. Discovering that the window was open, the man came to a halt. From what Calamity could make out, he possessed a sufficiently hefty build for her not to relish the prospect of tangling with him barehanded. Slowly and carefully, he started to ease upward the bottom half of the window; which, Calamity recollected bitterly, she had obligingly opened just before she had climbed into that dadblasted feather bed.

"No!" she thought. "Not *just* before!"

Between opening the window and climbing into bed, she had performed a natural function made necessary by consuming a bottle of wine and sev-

eral cups of coffee in Freddie Woods' private railroad car.

Unlike her armament, the item she had used during her last act before climbing into bed was at the
side where she now knelt. A grin of delight creased
Calamity's face as she thought of the elegant pot's
sturdy construction. Handled correctly, it ought to
make a mighty effective deterrent against the man
at the window.

So far the intruder at the window showed no sign
of knowing that his proposed victim was awake,
alert and no longer in bed. Ducking his head forward, he prepared to enter the room. Luckily the
second man had not unlocked the door. As long as
she could take the first cuss out of the game,
Calamity figured she ought to be able to reach her
more conventional weapons. Holding the carbine,
Colt or whip, she reckoned that she could then
show her visitors a real hospitable welcome.

Gripping the handle of the chamber-pot, she
drew it from beneath the bed. At any moment she
expected to hear the lock click and see the door
open. There was no time to lose if she hoped to
achieve her ambition regarding the big man.

Swiftly Calamity thrust herself erect and into
motion, darting alongside the bed and across the
room. She heard the lock snap open mingled with
a startled exclamation from the man on the ladder.

"She's awake, Otón!" the big intruder at the
window bawled.

Light flooded into the room as the door began to open. Calamity knew that there would not be time for her to reach the window and make the speaker a present of the chamberpot for a hat, then return to the bed and grab a firearm, before his companion cut in. So she did not try.

Coming to a halt, Calamity hurled the contents of the chamber-pot into the face of the man at the window. While less permanent than her original intention, the result proved almost as satisfactory. Expecting to hear the occupant of the room start screaming fit to waken the dead, the man had already begun to snatch his head and torso back through the window. Caught in the face by the flood of urine, which stung his eyes and half-blinded him, he jerked to the rear at an even greater speed. So fast, in fact, that Calamity did not have a chance to study his features for future reference.

Spitting out a flow of foul language, the man made his involuntary retreat with such force that he wrenched the top of the ladder away from the wall. Back it tilted until it stood almost perpendicular. Then it began to reverse its course. Aware of the ladder's flimsy construction, the man doubted if it would stand up to the impact. Even if it did, the girl in the room might not restrict herself to the mere contents of the chamber-pot for her next attack.

With that thought in mind, the man transferred

his hands' grip to the sides of the ladder. Jerking
his feet from the rungs which had supported them,
he started to slide down to safety. Before he had
gone far, the top of the ladder crashed into the edge
of the windowsill. Timber crackled as the center of
the ladder buckled under the combined effects of
the collision and his weight. Cursing even more
wildly as a splinter of wood spiked into the palm
of his right hand, the man fell. He landed with one
foot crushing the crown of the hat he had discarded before climbing to the window.

While falling, he heard a shouted curse, a shot
and a crash from above him. The combined sounds
would be enough to disturb the entire first floor
and some of the guests were certain to investigate.
Still cursing under his breath, he rubbed a hand
across his face and blinked the tears from his
smarting eyes. Then he turned and lurched hurriedly toward an alley between two of the buildings behind the hotel.

Satisfied with the big man's abrupt disappearance from the window, Calamity was granted no
time for self-congratulation. Turning her head, she
found that the door had opened sufficiently for her
to look straight at the second intruder. While they
remained staring at each other for only a moment,
her mind registered a few significant facts about
the figure in the doorway.

Being situated behind him, the passage's lights
threw his features into such heavy shadow that she

could not hope to identify him that way. Bare-headed, he had black hair and wore ordinary, undistinguishable range clothes. While his bandana, shirt and Levi's pants offered little clue to the nature of his employment, the high-heeled boots on his feet and their large-roweled spurs suggested connections with the cattle rather than railroad, freight-wagon, buffalo-hunting or other Western industries.

In his right hand he held a long-bladed knife from the empty sheath at the left of his gunbelt. There was a gun at the right side; an 1860 Army Colt with fancy Tiffany grips instead of the usual hand-fitting curved butt. The holster it rode in attracted Calamity's attention for three reasons: first, it hung on a slightly longer than usual belt loop; second, its tip was not fastened to the wearer's thigh; third, its bottom was open and the Colt's barrel extended an inch below it.

"Hijo de puta!" the man spat out, surprised to find himself confronted by the victim he had assumed to still be in bed.

Tossing the knife to his left hand, his right fist dropped to the Colt's butt. Fast and practiced though the move had been, he did not complete it by raising the gun from the holster, which failed to lull Calamity into a sense of false security. Having associated with several notable members of the fast-draw fraternity and listened to them discussing the tools of their trade, she knew plenty about the methods of carrying a gun to facilitate its rapid withdrawal from leather. Although it was the first of its kind she had seen, she had heard mention of the type of holster worn by the intruder. Such a rig offered one major advantage. Its user did not need to draw the revolver before he commenced to throw lead.

Thumb-cocking the Colt without drawing it, the man started to tilt up the bottom of the holster in Calamity's direction. The girl did not hesitate in her reaction. Pivoting around, she swung and hurled the chamber-pot across the room with all the strength in her powerful young body. During her tomboy childhood, Calamity had won the reputation of being the best rock-pitcher around Princeton, Missouri, and had lost little of her ability while growing up. However, her unconventional missile did not lend itself to accuracy. Even as it left her hand, she knew instinctively that she would not make a hit.

At the sight of the chamber-pot hurtling his way, the man responded involuntarily. Still gripping the hilt of the knife, his left hand hooked on to the edge of the door. He could not prevent himself jerking back and starting to draw the door between himself and the missile. In doing so, he turned the muzzle of his Colt out of line at the moment that he released his hold on the hammer. Flame spurted from the barrel and the detonation of the shot shattered the silence of the night. Then the chamber-pot struck against the upper edge of the door. Bursting apart by the force of the impact, it sprayed the man with fragments of broken pottery and caused him to accelerate his departure. He went knowing that his bullet had missed the girl.

Jerking the door closed, the man swiftly assessed the situation. The speed with which the girl had reacted did not spring out of fright or panic. Instead, she had moved throughout with a grim, dangerous purpose that gave the man a warning. If he continued to force his attentions upon the occupant of Room Fourteen, he was likely to meet with a noisy, violent resistance. Immediately after throwing the chamber-pot, she had started to dart toward the bed. Most likely she went to lay hands on some more lethal and effective weapon. So she must be prevented from using it. Releasing the butt of his Colt, his right hand flashed across to lock the door.

"Hey you!" yelled a male voice from along the passage, fortunately not in the direction of the stairs. "What're you up to?"

Swiveling his head around, the intruder saw the night-cap-topped face of a big, burly man peering cautiously around the door of Room Eighteen. Not only did the face show grim determination, but the barrel of a revolver extended beyond the door to prove he had the means of enforcing his demand for information. Pausing only to make sure his way was clear, the intruder spun on his heel and dashed to the stairs. More voices were raised along the passage and other doors opened. Ignoring them, the fleeing man bounded rapidly down the stairs.

Awakened by the disturbance from the first floor, Philpotter emerged from his office. At midnight he had followed his usual procedure by leaving the desk, removing his collar and tie, unbuttoning his vest and settling down to rest. He came out, bleary-eyed but filled with indignation, just in time to see the intruder leap down the remaining stairs.

"What——Who——?" Philpotter began.

It proved to be a mistake. Hearing the clerk's startled exclamation, the fleeing man turned his head that way and dropped his right hand to the gun's butt. No fighter, Philpotter adopted the wisest course and ducked hurriedly behind the desk. Frightened and quaking, the clerk remained in concealment and listened to the other man's running feet crossing the reception hall. Not until the thumping of the boot-heels died away along the sidewalk did Philpotter offer to raise his head. After making sure that the intruder really had left, he rose and hurried upstairs to investigate the cause of the upheaval to the hotel's normal peace and decorum.

Watching the door close as she darted across the room, Calamity reached the bed. She bounded over its end, landing and rolling across the mattress. Just before the door shut completely and blotted out the light, she stabbed forward her left hand to catch hold of the top of the carbine's barrel. Never had the little saddle-gun felt so comforting to her touch. She tossed it upward and caught the wooden fore-grip in her left hand. Then the right's fingers curled around the wrist of the butt. As she continued to roll from the bed, her right forefinger entered the trigger-guard and the other three found their way through the ring of the loading lever. Landing with her left leg bent and right knee upon the floor, she swung the brass butt-plate of the carbine to her right shoulder. Working the lever to feed a bullet from the magazine tube into the chamber, she took sight on the door.

Before she could squeeze the trigger, she noticed that the segmented strip of light below the door had become a whole line once more. That meant the man on the other side was no longer standing in her line of fire. Give him his due, though, he was a cool son-of-a-bitch. She had heard him lock the door as soon as he closed it.

For a moment Calamity considered shooting open the lock, then dismissed the notion as impractical and dangerous. Maybe the twenty-eight-grain load of powder in the .44 Winchester bullet lacked the long-range potential of a cigar-long buffalo rifle cartridge, but it packed enough power to pass through the lock, cross the passage and injure anybody unfortunate enough to be in its way in the room opposite. Nor would she be any better off if she burst open the lock. Clad only in a pair of drawers, she was not suitably attired to go chasing owlhoots around a fancy hotel—or any other place, come to that.

Shouts rang out in the passage as Calamity came to her feet. Then she remembered her other visitor. Turning, she darted across to the window. At the sight of the man's bulky figure heading for the alley, she knelt and rested her carbine on the windowsill. While not a particularly vindictive person, she figured that men ought to be dissuaded from the habit of attempting to break into harmless females' rooms. Being of a blunt and forthright disposition, she reckoned that a .44 bullet in the hide ought to make a mighty effective dissuader.

As Calamity only wanted to injure the man, she lined the carbine's sights with extra care. Just as her forefinger started to depress the trigger, a thunderous knocking on her door caused her to jerk around. The carbine spat viciously, but its muzzle no longer pointed in the required direction. Instead of plowing into the man's right hip, the bullet struck and threw a cloud of splinters from the corner of the left-side building.

Again the fist pounded on the door and a worried male voice bellowed, "Are you all right in there?"

A glance out the window told Calamity that the man had passed beyond any hope of immediate retribution. Straightening up, she turned and walked across the room. Approaching the door, she realized that she was no more suitably dressed for receiving visitors than for pursuing routed intruders.

Before she could formulate any solution to the problem, the matter was taken out of her hands. The lock clicked and the door burst open. Revolver in hand, a big, burly man lunged into the room. From the way he entered, he had experience in such important matters. Maybe not up to the standards of a trained peace officer, but adequate to offer him a chance of survival if there had been an enemy inside. Behind him, several other men clad in a variety of night-wear surged forward. They came to a halt, forced to it by the man in the lead. There was an air of hard-bitten authority about him that a night-cap and dressing-gown could not dispel. His entire attitude hinted that he was used to making decisions in a hurry—but he could be surprised.

Embarrassment swept the grim, purposeful frown from the man's face as he found himself confronted by a pretty, shapely girl who was naked to the waist, briefly clad below it and carried a smoking Winchester carbine. Exclamations of interest and approbation rose from the men who had followed him in.

"Are you all right, young lady?" the big man demanded.

"Sure," Calamity replied.

"Then we had better withdraw," the man stated, in tones that brooked no objection. Backing toward the door, he forced the others to leave. Turning his head so that he did not look at Calamity, he went on, "If I might make a suggestion, ma'am, you should put on a robe. The marshal or one of his deputies will be around to find out what's happening and he's sure to want to question you."

"I'll do just that," Calamity promised. "Leave the door open a mite so's I can find a match and light the lamp."

After the men had left, Calamity crossed to the wardrobe and took a box of matches from the pocket of her buckskin jacket. She lit the lamp and went to close the door, but could not follow the man's advice. Her normal way of life precluded the need for possessing such high-falutin' garments as a robe to wear over her sleeping clothes. However, she knew that he had been correct about the marshal or a deputy coming. So she slipped on her shirt and pants, then produced a pair of moccasins from her *parfleche*. Dressed adequately, if not conventionally, she walked from the room.

When she appeared in the passage, Calamity's wearing apparel drew almost as much comment from the men as had their first sight of her inside the room. Ignoring them, she went to where the big man stood talking to Philpotter.

"Do you get this sort of thing happening regular?" the girl inquired, looking at the clerk.

"This sort of thing?" Philpotter repeated.

"Fellers trying to bust into a gal's room from the door and the window," Calamity elaborated.

"There was another of them at the window?" asked the big man.

"Yep," agreed Calamity. "It was him I was trying to get a shot at just afore you bust in."

"Did you hit him?" the man wanted to know.

"Missed," answered the girl. "He lit out through the alley back of here."

"Would you know him again?" the man inquired.

"Nope," Calamity admitted. "I'll tell you one thing, though. He sure won't smell like a rose, way I got rid of him." She turned her attention to Philpotter again. "How's about it, friend. Do you get this sort of thing coming off regular?"

"Certainly not!" the clerk yelped indignantly. "It's the first time such a thing has happened here."

"*That* figures!" the girl declared, slapping the palms of her hands against her thighs in an exasperated manner. "Now you know why folks call me 'Calamity.' "

Chapter 3

A POOR, DEFENSELESS GAL LIKE ME

AT NINE O'CLOCK ON THE MORNING AFTER HER AR-
rival, Calamity Jane walked down the stairs to the
entrance hall of the Railroad House Hotel.
Philpotter was no longer at the desk and his tall,
lean, sour-faced replacement almost mirrored his
first reaction at the sight of the girl. Apart from not
earning the *parfleche* and carbine, she was dressed
as she had been on her arrival the previous night.

"Howdy," Calamity greeted amiably as she
reached the desk. "Where-at's Counselor Talbot's
office?"

"On Leicester Street," the clerk replied. "You
turn right, go by the newspaper office and take the

street alongside the stock-pens toward the railroad depot."

"Thanks," Calamity said, and decided to give the man some good news. "I'll likely be picking up my gear and pulling out after I've seen him."

"Which room would that be?" the clerk inquired frostily, but he looked a mite relieved to hear the information.

"Fourteen."

"Fourteen!—Oh! So you're the one—"

"If there's two of us, I've never seen the other," Calamity answered. "What'd your pard tell you about last night?"

"My par——?" the clerk began. "You mean Mr. Philpotter. He told me about the robbery, but I thought he was joking about the way you dre—— About how you were—— I mean about your clo——"

"Let's just leave it that he told you and save some spluttering," Calamity suggested, dropping the room key on the desk's top. "I don't suppose that deputy's been back to say he caught them two polecats?"

"No," the clerk replied, throwing a glance toward the open front doors.

"I wasn't expecting he would have," Calamity admitted. "See you around, feller. Don't let them two come back and wide-loop the desk from under you."

Taking out a white handkerchief as the girl

turned, the clerk shook it violently and mopped his brow. Calamity walked away from the desk, deciding that she would have been surprised if the deputy town marshal who had arrived to investigate the shooting had managed to locate and arrest the intruders.

On his arrival, the deputy had performed his duties efficiently enough; but there had been little he could do. After learning the cause of the commotion, he had requested the onlookers not directly concerned with the incident to return to their rooms. When all but Calamity, the big man in the nightcap—he had proved to be the senior cattle-buyer for a major Eastern meat-packing combine—and Philpotter had disappeared, the deputy had suggested that they should conclude their talk in the girl's room. There he had listened to her story. Although acting as nervous as a hen with a chicken-hawk circling its brood, Philpotter had laughed along with the important guest and the peace officer when Calamity described her use of the chamber-pot as a weapon. The clerk had even joined in the complimentary remarks made on the subject of the girl's courage and initiative. Those qualities, unfortunately, could not do anything further.

Regretfully Calamity had been forced to admit that she could not describe either intruder with any degree of certainty. The best she could manage was to state that the man at the window had been heavily built, probably tall and not wearing a hat. The other had been tallish, slim, with black hair, clad in cowhand clothes, carrying a knife and toting an Army Colt with Tiffany grips in what was known as a "half-breed" or "swivel" holster. His companion had called him what sounded like "Houghton" which hinted that he was of Anglo-Saxon birth.

The cattle-buyer and Philpotter had been able to add little more. They confirmed the girl's description of the physical appearance of the man in the passage. While both had noticed that he sported a drooping black mustache, neither could say what kind of features he had.

Borrowing a lantern from the desk clerk, the deputy had led the way outside and to the rear of the building. Finding the hat, they had examined it but it did not prove to be informative. It was a Stetson such as could be purchased from any general store west of the Mississippi River. Being stepped on by its bulky owner had squashed out any features that might have served as pointers to its place of origin.

The ladder had proved to have been stolen from alongside one of the buildings to the rear of the hotel. It had offered no clue to the person who had stolen it and the lantern's light had not been strong enough to illuminate the faint trace of blood where the splinter had spiked into the man's palm.

So there had been nothing to give the deputy a start in his search. Even the name Calamity had heard spoken did not help. Like all such towns, Mulrooney had a large, ever-changing, transient population. Many of the visitors did not even stay in town, but bedded down on the open range. A fair proportion of the floating population used whatever name came handiest. So the best the deputy could offer was that he would check through the marshal's reward posters and see if he could find a mention of a man called "Houghton" who matched the slimmer intruder's description. He did not offer much hope of success. Hotel sneak-thieves rarely rated the offer of a reward for their capture.

Being aware of the difficulties facing trail-end town peace officers, Calamity and the cattle-buyer had been satisfied with the deputy's offer. Philpotter had raised no objections, even if he thought them. It had always been his policy to pay lip-service to the desires of influential clients. If any of them had wondered why the intruders had selected Calamity's room as the start of their depredations, the point was not raised. Calamity put it down to no more than a lucky, or real unlucky—depending upon how one regarded it—coincidence.

Pausing at the door of the hotel, Calamity turned her head to look first right and then left. Having visited Mulrooney twice, she knew something of its geography but needed to get her bearings. While doing so, her left arm pressed against the side of the buckskin jacket and she felt the bulk of the envelope that she carried in the inside pocket. According to the lawyer in Topeka, Counselor Talbot would require to see proof of her identity. So she was taking along the necessary papers for his examination.

Just as she was starting to turn to the right, Calamity noticed a man standing across the street and studying her with obvious interest. Tall, lean, sharp-featured, he wore range clothes but had the appearance of a trail-end town loafer, the kind that hung around accepting the hospitality of the visitors and avoiding doing any work. That he looked at her intently came as no surprise to Calamity. Men had been doing it for so long that it had ceased to be a novelty or an embarrassment.

Ignoring the man, for she knew his kind too well to want any truck with them, Calamity strolled off along the sidewalk. She debated to herself whether to call at the Fair Lady Saloon before visiting the lawyer, but decided against it. Maybe after she had heard Counselor Talbot's news she would need advice. If so, Freddie Woods would be only too willing to give it.

Continuing along the street, Calamity paused to look at the display of firearms in the window of a gunsmith's store. While doing so, she became aware that the loafer was still opposite. Watching his reflection in the store's window, she saw him come to a halt, turn and stare along an alley. She stood for a moment before he looked over his shoulder in her direction. Then he swung his head around and resumed his scrutiny of the gap between the buildings.

"Now what's he following me for?" Calamity thought. "He looks too all-fired sweet 'n' noble to be figuring on interfering with a poor, defenseless gal like me. Especially in Mulrooney, in daylight, and with me packing a gun. Maybe it's just that he ain't never seed a gal's fills her pants as well's I do."

Satisfied that, no matter what his intentions might be, the loafer posed no threat to her, Calamity walked on. She went by the newspaper office and turned down the street that flanked the stock-pens. Keeping to the sidewalk, she looked across the street at the pens and the longhorn steers they held awaiting shipment East. She thought admiringly of the grit and tenacity required to drive the half-wild animals all the way from Texas and remembered that the bell-hop had mentioned one particular outfit was coming. She hoped that her business would not take her out of town before the OD Connected trail drive arrived.

For some reason, all the work being done around the pens took place on the opposite side to where Calamity walked. The buildings flanking the sidewalk also appeared to be deserted. Looking ahead, she could see another street running at right angles to the one she followed. That would be

Leicester Street and somewhere along it she would find Counselor Talbot's office.

Two men stepped from an alley at the end of the building which Calamity was approaching. They looked in her direction, but she formed the impression that their attention was centered on something, or somebody, behind her. At first glance, they appeared to be an ordinary enough pair of trail-end town visitors, but not the kind one would expect to see together. One of them, by his dress, hailed from north of Kansas and the other clearly came from very far south of the State. Leaving the north-country man, the second of the pair crossed to hook his rump on the hitching mil in front of the next building.

Their behavior struck the girl as just a mite peculiar. While not vain, she knew that she had a good figure and dressed in a manner to show it off. Yet, after their first glance, neither man turned his eyes toward Calamity. In fact they seemed to be avoiding meeting her gaze just a mite too carefully.

Partly because one saw so few of his kind in Kansas, Calamity gave the seated man a close scrutiny before looking at his companion who leaned against the building's wall. Tall, slender yet wiry, he had a clean-shaven Latin face that a thin, cruel mouth prevented from being handsome. The hat he wore was no Stetson. Its pointed crown, silver concha-decorated band and wide, circular brim had their origin south of the Rio Grande. So did the waist-long black jacket with silver filigree patterning, white, frilly-fronted shirt, string bow-tie, tight-legged, wide-bottomed trousers and high-heeled boots with large-rowelled spurs attached to them. As might be expected from such a man, he carried a fighting knife sheathed on the left side of his gunbelt. The position in which he sat prevented Calamity from seeing either his gun or its holster.

From the Mexican, Calamity turned her gaze to his white companion. She had walked closer and began to notice some disturbingly significant details about him.

Taller and heavier than the Mexican, the second man also lacked the other's finery. Nothing about his wolfskin coat, tartan shirt, dark trousers tucked into flat-heeled boots or gunbelt was new. The same did not apply to his hat; that was brand-new. Although he had a fast-draw holster tied down on his right thigh, it did not hold a gun. Instead, an Army Colt was thrust into his waistband, its butt pointed to the front for a cross-hand draw. The reason for the empty holster and gun's position probably stemmed from the fact that he had a dirty piece of rag wrapped around his right hand. Surly-featured and unshaven, his eyes had a red-rimmed, bloodshot appearance that could have been the result of drinking hard the previous night—or having the contents of a chamber-pot thrown into his face.

Taken with the state of the man's eyes, the

brand-new hat and the bandaged hand suggested certain unpleasant possibilities to Calamity. A feller who slid hurriedly down a ladder, especially one in the process of breaking, might easily tear open his palm on a splinter. That jasper from her window had left his hat behind and would need to replace it if he hoped to avoid drawing attention to himself.

Of course the facts might amount to no more than a coincidence; but Calamity felt disinclined to take bets on it.

As if wanting to sweep any lingering doubts from the girl's mind, the Mexican stood up and faced her. Calamity's eyes dropped swiftly to his right thigh. Before raising them again, she schooled her features into lines of indifference and hid her concern. The Colt at his side had the distinctively shaped Tiffany grips and the end of its barrel protruded from the open toe of the holster.

Still continuing to walk toward the pair, Calamity rapidly marshaled her facts. She did not like the answers she came up with. The assailant inside the hotel had worn ordinary range clothes and, according to the cattle-buyer, had sported a drooping black mustache. Clothes could be changed and a mustache shaved off. The Mexican's hair was black and he might have removed the facial growth to prevent himself being recognized during his stay in Mulrooney.

Which raised another interesting, maybe even

vital point. Why had the two men remained in
town and what brought them to stand on the sidewalk ahead of her? The attempted robbery at the
hotel did not rate as such a serious crime that they
needed to remove a witness who might be able to
identify them. Nor had Calamity's treatment of
them been sufficiently drastic for the pair to risk
arrest by hunting her up in search of revenge.

And that thought brought up another. If the pair
should be vindictive enough to be looking for
evens, how did they know where to find her? How
did they recognize her, come to that? Unless they
had seen her entering the Railroad House, her
clothes would not identify her. Female guests at
that hotel did not dress in her style. Yet she felt
sure that their presence on the deserted street had
not come about by accident.

One thing was plain to Calamity. She must not
let the pair suspect that she had recognized them.
Maybe if she could get up close enough, with them
figuring that she did not know them, she could escape from the position they had her in.

"You boys fixing on making a gal take to the
street to get by?" Calamity asked, hoping that her
voice did not sound as tensed-up as she felt.

Instead of moving aside, the two men looked her
over with cold eyes. Then the Mexican seemed to
glance at something behind her, but Calamity figured that she had been around too long to fall for
that old trick. Instead of looking to the rear for the

non-existent danger, she continued to approach the pair and watched for any hostile move or gesture.

"Is your name 'Canary,' gal?" demanded the big man.

"Do I *look* like a canary?" Calamity countered, but the question had started a further train of thought leaping through her head.

"It's her for certain, Job," the Mexican stated.

"You'd know, Otón," the big man growled. "Way you told it, you saw her real good last night."

"I don't get it," Calamity began, right hand turning palm-outward and moving surreptitiously in the direction of her Navy Colt.

The words chopped off as she heard the faint sound of a footstep behind her. Faint only because the person making it was stepping real careful and avoiding making undue noise, not because some distance separated him from the girl.

Anger blazed up inside Calamity, driving the thoughts of how they knew her name into oblivion. For the second time in less than twenty-four hours she had committed a serious error of tactics. Concentrating on the two yahoos blocking her path, she had clean forgotten that skinny-gutted loafer who had dogged her trail since she left the hotel. In fact, his presence behind her answered some of the problems which had troubled her. He must have been following, soft-footed as a cat, to point her out to the pair.

Only he had made his presence known just a mite too soon. His pards were still about twelve feet away, beyond arms' reach. Seeing the girl's right hand approaching the ivory butt of the holstered Colt, the loafer lunged forward. He wrapped his arms about her upper torso from the rear, drawing her toward him. Instantly his companions let out curses and sprang forward.

Calamity had learned how to handle such sneaky attacks, as she proceeded to demonstrate. Allowing her captor to pull her in his direction, she waited until she felt his body against her spine. Then she snapped back her head as hard as she could propel it. The base of Calamity's skull rammed with considerable force into the center of the man's face. Red fires of agony seemed to burst inside the man's head at the savage impact. With a howl of pain, he released the girl and staggered backward. Blood gushed between his fingers as he clasped his hands to his face.

Despite having removed one threat to her well-being, Calamity knew that she was a long, long way from being out of danger. Job and the Mexican came toward her, their expressions warning her that they had no harmless intent. Of the two, Otón moved the faster, drawing ahead of his companion.

Having freed herself from the loafer's restraining hands, Calamity once more reached for her gun. Tough she might be, and well able to hold up her own end in a hair-yanking, anything-goes, rough-house brawl with another girl; but her assailants were not girls. She figured that her best chance against the two men would be to get out the old Navy Colt and start burning powder. In addition to halting the Mexican, the sound of the shots would attract attention to her dangerous situation. The opportunity to do it was not granted to her.

Gliding forward with the speed of a weasel chasing a rabbit, Otón stabbed out both his hands. Closing his fingers on the lapels of her jacket, he wrenched them apart and down over her shoulders. Although the jacket had not been fastened, it still gripped her arms and prevented her from completing her draw. Once again the girl found herself partially trapped and countered the move in a fast, efficient manner.

Instead of trying to retreat, which Otón expected her to do, Calamity moved to meet him. With her upper arms pinioned, she could draw neither Colt nor whip. Unfortunately for the Mexican, her legs were still free. A point which she proceeded to take rapid and devastating advantage of. Going in as close as she could, Calamity drove up her right leg. Powered by a set of shapely, but well-developed muscles, her knee drove between Otón's legs. It caught him right where it would do the most good, for Calamity, if not for him. If she had been able to get in closer and put more force behind the attack, she would have tumbled her victim in numb, helpless agony to the ground. Instead, her knee arrived hard enough to make him gasp a gush of garlic-scented breath into her face as he released the jacket and fell back a pace.

Having taken two of her attackers out of the game, if only briefly, Calamity's luck ran out. Slower on his feet than Otón, Job proved sufficiently fast for the girl's undoing. Elbowing the Mexican aside and ignoring the loafer who stood glaring wildly at the blood that splashed from his nostrils on to his upturned palms, Job launched a punch in the girl's direction. She saw the blow coming just a moment too late. Even as she tried to duck under it, the burly man's knotted fist crashed against the side of her jaw. Instantly Calamity's world seemed to explode into brilliant flashes of light. She seemed to be falling through space, then her shoulder collided with something hard and unyielding. After that, everything went black for her.

Watching Calamity pitch sideways, ram her shoulder into the wall of the building and collapse, Job followed her. Bending down, he took hold of her jacket and started to raise her.

"Let's get her into the alley afore——" the big man began.

Leaning against the hitching rail and rubbing at the place where Calamity's knee had struck him, Otón shook his head.

"She'll have the papers we want on her. Get them now, just in case somebody's seen us. We may have to run for it before we've done the rest of our work."

"Be best," grunted Job and reached under Calamity's jacket. Producing the envelope, he lifted the flap and looked at the contents. "These're 'em. Now let's——"

"Leave her to me!" the lanky man screeched, drawing his revolver with a blood-smeared hand. "I'll kill her now and save you doing it!"

Chapter 4

WAS THE LETTER IMPORTANT?

THE TEXAS COWHAND STRIDING ALONG LEICESTER Street looked exceptionally young and naïve. Especially in view of the weapons about his person. A Winchester Model of 1866 rifle dangled almost negligently from his right hand. Walnut handle pointing forward, an old Colt Dragoon hung in a low "cavalry twist-hand" open-topped holster at the right side of his belt, and an ivory-hilted James Black bowie knife graced the sheath at the left.

Six foot in height, slender yet conveying an impression of strength and untiring energy, he had raven-black hair. In fact, black might have been his leitmotif. All his clothing, low-crowned, wide-brimmed Stetson, tight-rolled bandana, shirt, calf-skin vest, trousers, boots, gunbelt even, was of that somber hue. His deeply tanned face had almost babyishly innocent features that were belied by the reckless glint in his red-hazel eyes. Those eyes would have warned a stranger that this was no bald-faced boy trying to impress people. None of the town's original inhabitants, or many folk who knew the lands west of the Mississippi River would have even started to think it. He walked with a long, free stride, seeming to glide rather than step. His whole being told that there was here a young *man*, born and brought to maturity in the range country. In his time, he had seen much of life and something of sudden, violent death.

That tall, baby-faced Texan had seen his first light of day in the village of the *Pehnane*—by translation, Wasp, Quick-Stinger—Comanche Indians. Born to a wild Irish-Kentuckian and the only daughter of Chief Long Walker's French-Creole *pairaivo*, favorite wife, he had been given the name of Loncey Dalton Ysabel by the band's medicine man. His mother had died in childbirth and, in the traditional Comanche way—his father being away much of time on the family's business of mustanging or smuggling—he was raised by his maternal grandfather. A noted war leader in the Dog Soldier lodge, Long Walker had taught the boy all those things a *Pehnane* warrior must know.* Skill of riding came early and he reached considerable proficiency, for the Comanche were horse-Indians second to none. Equally important and well-learned had been the ability to handle weapons; which every *Nemenuh*† brave-heart needed to know if he was to be worthy of the name.

By the time he had reached his fifteenth birthday, the Ysabel Kid—as he was known among such Texans as he came into contact with—could handle a rifle and show the deadly sighting skill of a Kentucky hill man. His skill in the use of another weapon had already brought him the man-name *Cuchilo* among the *Pehnane*; the word was Spanish for Knife. While not fast, in the accepted Western sense of the word, he considered himself adequate in the use of his old Dragoon Colt. He could follow tracks and read the message they told as if it had been printed as a story in a book. With greater ease, in fact, for his white man's schooling had been fragmentary. Few men of either the white or red race could equal him at silent movement, hiding undetected or locating concealed enemies. All three subjects had formed a part of his *Pehnane* higher education.

The War between the States had come in time to prevent the Kid from having to choose whether to

---

* Told in *Comanche.*

† Nemenuh: the People, the Comanches' name for themselves.

support the white or Comanche sides of his bloodline. Accompanying his father, he had joined Mosby's Raiders and won the Grey Ghost's commendation by his skill as a scout. Then the Confederate States' Government had found a better use for the Ysabel family's talents. Sam Ysabel and his son had been returned to Texas, where they had collected cargoes, run through the U.S. Navy's blockade into neutral Matamoros and delivered them to the authorities north of the Rio Grande. During that period, the Kid had increased the fame he had been building along the bloody border before the War.

Bushwhack lead had cut down Sam Ysabel shortly after peace came. While on a vengeance hunt for his father's killers, the Kid had met up with Dusty Fog and Mark Counter.* In addition to achieving his revenge, he had helped the Rio Hondo gun wizard, Dusty Fog, to complete successfully a mission on which the possible peace of the United States depended.†

At a loose end, with smuggling no longer holding any interest for him, the Kid had accepted Dusty's offer of employment with the OD Connected ranch. Not merely as a working cowhand but to be one of the floating outfit. Usually a float-

---

* Dusty Fog's and Mark Counter's stories are told in the author's floating outfit books.

† Told in *The Ysabel Kid*.

ing outfit consisted of half a dozen top-hands who roamed their spread's far ranges as a kind of mobile ranch crew. Things did not work out that way in the OD Connected's case. The hand-picked elite of a crew noted as first-class cattle-workers and fighters, the floating outfit had frequently been sent to help friends of their boss, Ole Devil Hardin, who found themselves in trouble. Less of a cowhand than his companions, the Kid had found his niche by putting to good use his *Pehnane* education.

On the whole, though, the citizens of the Lone Star State might have counted themselves fortunate that such a potentially dangerous young man had accepted honest employment instead of, as might easily have happened, taking to riding the owlhoot trails.

Sent ahead of the OD Connected trail herd on urgent business for his boss, the Kid had reached Mulrooney that morning. He had taken advantage of a long-standing offer by leaving his white stallion and three-horse relay in Freddie Woods' stable. Carrying a large sum of money strapped about his middle, he toted along his rifle as a precaution against theft. Looking diagonally across Leicester Street, he located the shingle which hung outside Counselor Talbot's office. There was a fair number of people walking along the other side, so he did not cross over. The stock-pens commenced beyond the side-street that he approached. Wanting to find the extent of competition for his spread's herd, he intended to stroll along the side of the pens until opposite the lawyer's office.

Glancing idly along the side-street, the Kid saw something that drove all such thoughts from his head. Since becoming a member of the floating outfit, he had twice found himself wearing the badge of a deputy town marshal. The second time had been in Mulrooney and he still retained an honorary official status.* Even without those episodes, he would not have ignored the sight that met his eyes.

Just as the Kid came on the scene, Job had emptied Calamity's pocket. The burly man's comments did not cover the forty yards separating him from the Kid, but the loafer's screeched-out suggestion made it. That and the sight of the drawn revolver caused the Kid to halt and face the men. He neither knew nor cared who their victim might be, but was certain that the lean man must be stopped before he committed a cold-blooded murder.

"Drop the gun!" barked the Kid, advancing along the sidewalk.

Having no desire to become involved in a shooting fracas at that moment, especially against a man armed with a rifle and beyond safe revolver-range, Job hurriedly stuffed Calamity's letter into his jacket's inside pocket.

---

*The first occasion is told in *Quiet Town*.

"Get the hell out of it, Otón!" he snarled urgently. "Leave Smith to it!"

Advice which the Mexican was only too willing to obey. They had been sent to Mulrooney for a purpose and had only partially carried it out. However, he did not intend to get killed trying to do the rest. Especially when the rage-blinded loafer might complete their work for them.

Oblivious of the fact that his companions were beating a hasty retreat into the alley, Smith realized that another factor had entered the game. The Kid's words caused the loafer to look in his direction. Transferring some of the hatred he felt for Calamity to the interloper, Smith brought his weapon to shoulder level and at arm's length. Taking a quick aim, he cut loose with a shot in the Kid's direction.

It proved to be a costly mistake, despite the loafer displaying a fair amount of skill in the fast alignment of a revolver's sights. However, a distance of forty yards was far from the ideal range over which to use a handgun. Going up against a man of the Kid's ability, when the latter was armed with his Winchester, was suicidal under those conditions.

Not that the loafer did badly. In fact, he might have made a hit if he had been dealing with a slower man than the Kid. Seeing that Smith did not intend to obey his order, the Kid took evasive action. Long before he had taken a badge as a peace officer, he had learned that billing into such a situation required an instant readiness to handle reprisals. So, even as he shouted the order—a thing he would not have done before he met Dusty Fog—and saw Smith turn the revolver in his direction, he was already bringing the rifle into a firing position.

Swiftly the Kid sank into a kneeling posture. Nor did he move an instant too soon. Along the sidewalk, Smith's revolver cracked and its bullet passed through the space just vacated by the Kid's head. More than that, the man cocked his weapon as its recoil kicked the muzzle into the air. There was a smooth precision about the move which warned the Kid that the loafer possessed a dangerous proficiency in the use of a revolver.

Certainly sufficient for the Kid to be disinclined to take chances. Moving as if of its own volition, the rifle cradled its butt against the right shoulder of the black shirt. Instinctively the Kid's left elbow came to rest on his raised left knee. The moment his right knee settled on the planks of the sidewalk, the Kid was setting his sights. His right forefinger caressed the trigger and he felt the rifle recoil against his collar-bone. Smoke swirled momentarily before him and, as it whisked away, he saw the loafer rear back. Caught in the head by the Kid's bullet, the man tossed aside his revolver. He spun around, struck the hitching rail and fell over it to land limply on his back in the street.

Blurring the loading lever through its cycle, the Kid ejected the empty case and replaced it with a cartridge from the magazine tube. With that precaution taken, ignoring the shouts which rose from Leicester Street and across the stock-pens, he sprang forward. Running toward the alley, with the intention of catching the other two men, he received his first clear view of their victim.

Having met Calamity outside Elkhorn, Montana, the Kid recognized her immediately. There might be other young women who wore male clothing in the West, although few of them would appear so dressed on the streets of a big town like Mulrooney, but the coiled bull-whip on her belt identified Calamity almost before he had seen her face.

"Anyways," the Kid thought as he skidded to a halt. "It'd have to be that danged fool Calamity. No other gal'd get herself into a fix like this."

Resting his rifle against the wall, he knelt by the girl. Despite his thought, concern showed on his Indian-dark face; even if it would have taken a real close friend to detect the emotion. Gently he raised the girl and supported her back against his raised left knee. From what he could see, Calamity had been lucky when Job had struck her. Instead of going head-first into the wall, she had still been sufficiently erect for her shoulder to take the impact. So she had avoided suffering a serious injury and was already groaning her way back to consciousness.

Footsteps thudded from two directions as people ran toward where the Kid supported Calamity. Turning his head to look at the loafer's body, he saw several men approaching fast along a space between two sets of stock-pens. He forgot his intention of pursuing the other two men and turned his attention back to the girl. Much to his relief, he saw her eyes flicker open. No mutual recognition showed in them. Letting out a muffled gurgle that the Kid guessed was meant to be some mighty explosive profanity, she tried to grab at the indistinct shape in front of her.

"Easy there, Calam gal!" the Kid suggested gently, catching hold of her wrists with his hands and not sorry that the blow had left her in a weakened condition or that the jacket still entangled her biceps. "Take it easy, you *loco* she-male you. They've lit out and this here's me."

Slowly the dazed expression cleared from the girl's eyes. Looking at her rescuer, she stopped struggling. Still letting her lean against his knee, the Kid returned the jacket to its correct position.

"L-Lon——!" Calamity croaked. "What—Where——" She placed a hand on her jaw. "Ooh!"

"How's it feel, gal?" asked the Kid.

"Like my son-of-a-bitching jaw's busted,"

Calamity muttered thickly as she tenderly fingered the impact point of Job's fist. Then she glared around in fury and tried to rise. "Where're they at?"

"Two of 'em took off, running like a Nueces steer," the Kid replied. "The other's on the street there, but don't pay him no never-mind. He's not going any place right now."

In the lead of the crowd attracted by the shooting, a pair of Texas cowhands came to a halt. They had known the Kid when he wore a badge in Mulrooney and the taller man asked what had happened.

"Three *pelados* set on Calamity here," the Kid answered. "Why'd they do it to you, Calam gal?"

"Damned if I know," the girl began. Then she grabbed at the left side of the jacket and discovered that its breast pocket was empty. "Hey! Did I drop a letter while I was fussing with them?"

"Don't see it arou——" the Kid started to say. "One of them was putting an envelope in his pocket when they lit out!"

"They must've wide-looped mine then!" Calamity yelled indignantly, ignoring the pain it caused to her jaw.

"Take after 'em, boys!" the Kid requested, looking at the cowhands. "One's a big jasper and the other's dressed like a Mexican. Watch 'em, they look like they can use their guns."

"So can we," the shorter Texan pointed out and

sprang into the mouth of the alley followed by his companion.

"Was the letter important?" the Kid inquired, helping Calamity to rise while the onlookers milled around uncertainly.

"Not 'specially. It told who I am."

"Don't *you* know who you are?"

"Of course I know, you blasted knob-head!" the girl yelped and her face twisted in a spasm of pain. "Damn and blast you, you grinning *Pehnane* slit-eye, you made me hurt my poor aching jaw. Them papers was to show to Counselor Talbot."

"All right, folks," said a polite, yet authoritative voice from the rear of the crowd. "Open up and let us through!"

Obediently the assembled people moved aside. Not only did Marshal Kail Beauregard make the request but he was accompanied by three deputies and Mulrooney's well-respected lady mayor.

Six foot tall, well-made, ruggedly handsome, Beauregard wore the dress of a professional gambler and belted a low-hanging Army Colt. He had been the man selected as best suited to handle the varied, often conflicting personalities to visit the town. The residents had no reason to regret Freddie Woods' choice. Taking over from Dusty Fog, Beauregard had continued to uphold the high standards of honesty and fair dealing established by the Rio Hondo gun wizard in his brief term of office.

Without wasting time, the marshal set about his work. Indicating the body crumpled on the street, he asked, "You, Kid?"

"Me," the Kid confirmed and picked up his rifle. "It seemed like a good thing to do at the time, seeing's how he was set on shooting Calam here when I showed up and he tried to turn his gun on me."

"Oh! Hey, Calamity," Beauregard greeted, eyeing the girl from head to toe and adopting a tone that she had heard from more than one friend whom she had visited when he was employed as a peace officer. "You're sure livening up my town."

"I knowed it!" Calamity wailed, turning to the grave-faced lady mayor. "I just knowed I'd get the blame!"

An inch taller than Calamity, although looking more with her raven black hair taken up in an elegant pile on top of her head, Freddie Woods left the girl far behind in the beauty stakes. As always when attending to the affairs of mayor, or going about the town on business, Freddie wore a stylish black two-piece outfit that met with approval— and some envy—from even the most strait-laced of the "good" womenfolk. That her clothes showed off a magnificent figure could not be helped. The seamstress had yet to be born who could make clothes to conceal the curves with which nature had endowed the Right Honourable Lady Winifred Besgrave-Woodstole, to give her her full and correct title.

"They do call you 'Calamity,' " Freddie pointed out, her accents upper-class British. "There must be a reason for it."

"If there is," Calamity sighed. "I sure never asked for it."

Returning from the alley, breathing hard, the two cowhands stated that there had been no sign of Calamity's assailants.

"Figured it'd be best to come back and leave the marshal do the going around and asking folks," the shorter cowhand commented.

"Thanks," Beauregard answered, accepting the words as a tribute. There were trail-end towns where Texas cowhands would not have credited the local peace officers with the desire or ability to perform such a duty. "What happened, Calamity?"

"It was that pair from the hotel," the girl replied, touching her jaw gently.

"They come after you again?"

"Sure, Marshal. And, way I see it now, they was after me last night as well."

"Can you ask Calamity the questions somewhere that she can sit down, Kail?" Freddie put in. "That must have been quite a crack one of them gave her."

"Why sure," Beauregard agreed. "I'm sorry, Calam. Walt, see to things here. Stan, Irv, take these two Texas gents with you and look for——"

"A big, heavy-set bastard with a brand new

black hat, wolf-skin jacket, tartan shirt, black pants tucked into flat-heeled boots. His holster's empty, but he's got a gun in his waistband. Right hand's bandaged and his eyes're a mite bloodshot for some reason I wouldn't know about," Calamity continued for the marshal, bringing chuckles from the deputies who had heard of her actions the previous night. "The other's a tall, lean Mexican, *without* a mustache. I'll bet he's walking a mite scrunched up, though."

"How come?" asked the taller cowhand.

"I let him feel my knee-bone," the girl answered.

"Where?" inquired one of the deputies.

For a moment Calamity was on the verge of telling him. Then she saw Freddie watching her and assumed an expression of innocence almost equaling the Kid's.

"Let's just say some place 'tween his neck and his knee," she replied. "Happen you come across 'em, watch the Mex. He don't need to pull his gun afore he starts to throw lead."

At that moment Freddie and the Kid saw the tall, well-padded, excellently dressed figure of Counselor Talbot coming through the crowd. While Beauregard went to look at the loafer's body, Freddie and the Kid intercepted the lawyer.

"Got a letter for you, Counselor," the Kid greeted.

"May we use your chambers, Charles?" Freddie interrupted, and pointed to the girl. "The marshal wants to question Calamity and she has to come and see you."

"*You* do, young lady?" Talbot asked, looking puzzled as the girl joined them.

"Sure," Calamity agreed. "I'm Martha Jane Canary, Counselor." Reaching across with her right hand, she rubbed the material over the empty pocket. "Trouble being, I can't come right out with any papers to prove it."

Chapter 5

THE ANSWER IS IN HOLLICK CITY

"Hope you don't mind, Freddie," the Kid said as they followed Calamity, Beauregard and Talbot toward the lawyer's office, "I left my hosses in your stable. I didn't see nobody around to ask——"

"It's all right," Freddie smiled. "How soon will the herd be here?"

"A week, ten days, I'd say. Dusty sent me ahead with a letter from Ole Devil and I've been covering fifty miles a day to their fifteen to twenty."

"It's fortunate for Calamity that Dusty sent you. I was just coming to see Charles Talbot, with Kail and his deputies, when we heard the shots."

"If you've all got business with him, along of Calam 'n' me, he's in for a right busy morning."

"My business wasn't all that urgent," Freddie admitted, dropping her voice so that the others would not hear. "But I couldn't resist the temptation to come. I'm rather intrigued by why Charles should want to see Calamity."

"They do say all women-folk's naturally nosy," the Kid remarked with a grin.

"I'll treat that remark with the contempt it deserves," Freddie smiled, then became serious as Calamity's words drifted back to them.

"I still reckon they're the same pair's tried to bust into my room last night, Kail!" the girl was insisting.

"You said that the big feller called his pard 'Houghton,' " Beauregard objected. "That's not a Mexican name."

"Maybe he was shouting to that skinny-gutted cuss the Kid dropped," Calamity suggested.

"Was he there? The dead feller, I mean."

"If he was, I never saw him. It wasn't him at the door, I'm sure of that. Should he've been there?"

"I wouldn't know," Beauregard admitted. "Looked him over, back there. His name's 'Smith,' for what that proves. Been around town for a couple of months now. Never did a lick of work, but always seemed to have money. That sort of feller always interests me. Never heard him called 'Houghton,' or anything other than 'Smith.' "

"There must've been somebody born called

'Smith,' " Calamity replied. "Anyways, I'm sure that big jasper said 'Houghton.' "

"If he did, his pard at the hotel wouldn't be a Mexican," Beauregard pointed out. "In which case, the two who jumped you aren't the same pair as at the hotel."

"I wouldn't be sure of that, Kail," Freddie put in. "It could have been 'Otón', O-t-ó-n, he said. That's Spanish for the name 'Otto.' "

"You could have it, Freddie," the Kid enthused, surprised to discover that she spoke Spanish.

"It could've been," Calamity agreed, eyeing the marshal triumphantly. "I just knew I didn't have two sets of folks riled up at me."

"You wouldn't want to bet on *that*, would you?" drawled the Kid.

"So you think they were after you for that letter they took?" asked Beauregard, before Calamity could give the Kid an appropriate answer.

"That's what I reckon," Calamity replied.

"Was it valuable, Miss Canary?" Talbot asked, having followed the conversation without joining in it up to that point.

"Shuckens no!" the girl answered. " 'Least, not to anybody else. It was only the stuff I showed you on the train last night, Freddie. My birth certificate and a letter Maw left with the sisters, telling who I am and why she was doing it. They weren't worth a plugged nickel."

They had reached the door to the lawyer's office

by that time. The conversation lapsed until Talbot had escorted them into his comfortably furnished private room and seated them around his large, impressive desk. Watching him, Freddie knew that something was troubling the lawyer. With his visitors settled, Talbot gave a cough which Freddie recognized as expressing perturbation.

"I'm afraid you're wrong about the papers, Miss Canary," the lawyer said. "If they establish your identity, they would have been comparatively valuable."

"How come?" the girl asked, sinking with relief into the comfortable chair.

"Well," Talbot replied, looking more worried, "I'm not sure that I can divulge——"

Having the frontier man's distrust for manipulators of the law, even when he knew them to be as trustworthy as Talbot, the Kid bristled indignantly and growled, "Losing them papers don't change who Calam is. If you could've told her what it's about after you'd read 'em, I don't see why you can't do it now."

"If it will help, Charles," Freddie went on. "I saw the papers last night, and read them. I'm willing to swear an affidavit as to their contents."

"I don't doubt that Miss Canary is telling the truth, Freddie," Talbot answered. "However, in a court of law, your ability to recognize or detect forged documents might be called into question."

"Feller who did the calling wouldn't do it twice,

was we around," the Kid remarked in that gentle, mild-sounding tone so well known and feared in the Rio Grande border country.

"Let's hear Charles out," Freddie smiled, "shall we, Lon?"

"I've no objection to telling Miss Canary the reason for her being asked to come here," Talbot declared. "But——"

"If it's confidential, we'll leave until you've told her," Freddie promised and the marshal nodded his agreement.

"That's up to Miss Canary," Talbot stated.

"Stay put, all of you," Calamity requested, eyeing the open cigar-box on the lawyer's desk with interest. There had been one like it in front of her all through the interview with Grosvenor, but he did not offer her a smoke from it. "If whatever you've got to tell me ties in with those two yahoos stealing the letter, Kail's going to hear about it anyways; and they're all my friends. Tell ahead, Counselor."

For a moment Calamity thought that Talbot was going to offer the cigar-box around. Instead, he opened the desk's drawer, fumbled inside and produced a sheet of paper. Calamity wondered if all the legal profession were so all-fired stingy with their cigars.

"Three weeks ago," Talbot announced, tapping the paper, "I received this letter from an old law-school classmate of mine, Orde Endicott. He is in practice at Hollick City, over in Nebraska, and asked me to assist him. It seems that your father bought the Rafter C ranch in your name in Hollick County——"

"My pappy owns a ranch?" Calamity gasped.

"No," Talbot corrected. "*You* own the ranch. The deeds to it, properly registered, are in your name. So, legally, you own the Rafter C."

"Whee doggie!" Calamity ejaculated. "If that don't beat all. So your pard asked you to find me for him?"

"Not exactly," the lawyer answered. "He said that arrangements had already been made for Pinkerton's Agency to look for you. My share in the affair was to offer you the sum of six thousand dollars for the ranch."

"That's a tidy sum of money," Calamity remarked.

"Or nowheres near enough, depending on the ranch," the Kid went on.

Freddie saw the worry and embarrassment grow on Talbot's face and began to guess at the cause of the emotions. Once again Talbot coughed. Then he threw an imploring glance at the beautiful English girl and turned back to Calamity.

"I'm afraid, as things now stand, that I can't make you the offer, Miss Canary. While I accept your *bona fides*——"

"I never knowed I had any of 'em," Calamity put in. "What in hell're they?"

"While I accept that you are Robert Howard Canary's daughter, Martha Jane," Talbot explained, looking like a man sitting on a powder keg that was about to explode, "I can't hand over the money for the ranch without seeing documentary proof that it is so."

"Is that the legal law?" demanded the Kid, scowling across the desk and looking as mean as a *Pehnane* Dog Soldier on the war trail.

"I'm afraid it is," the lawyer confirmed.

"Then I'm pleased as hell's I've never been——!" the Texan blazed.

"I don't know what you're starting to paw and beller for," Calamity interrupted. "Seeing's how I'm not fixing to sell out anyways."

"You're not?" Talbot asked, looking relieved.

"Nope. Way I see it, if pappy bought me a ranch, least I can do is go over to Hollick City and take a look at it."

"It won't do you any good," Talbot warned. "You can't establish your identity there any more than you can here."

"And it might be dangerous," Beauregard went on. "If you're right about them two fellers being after your letter, and it looks like you are, they'll not take kind to you showing up in Hollick City."

"*I* don't take kind to what they done to me out

on the street!" Calamity replied, then winced and touched her jaw delicately with a fingertip.

"How'd they know where to find you, Calam?" the Kid asked.

"Now that's a thing's's been bothering me," the girl admitted. "The Railroad House'd be the last place anybody's knowed me'd expect to find me in."

"They didn't know *you*," Freddie pointed out. "If they had known you as Calamity Jane, I doubt if they would have tried to break into your room last night."

"Perhaps I can explain that," Talbot remarked. "According to his letter, Orde Endicott was under the impression that you had been left in the East by your parents. He didn't know that the young lady he sought was Calamity Jane."

Always quick to jump to conclusions, Calamity snorted and asked, "You mean that your law-wrangling pard sent them two jaspers after me?"

"I didn't say that!" Talbot protested. "As far as I know, Orde Endicott is an honest, upstanding member of the Bar."

"Just how far do you know about him, Counselor?" inquired the Kid.

"He was the brightest member of our class and had a brilliant career as a defense attorney in the East."

"Yet he wound up hanging his shingle in a one-hoss Nebraska cow-town?"

"I believe he moved out there for health reasons," Talbot answered, looking uncomfortable.

"Right now," Beauregard said firmly, before the Kid could speak again, "I'm more interested in those two fellers who jumped Calamity. Did they follow on the train, or from the depot, do you reckon, Calam?"

"They didn't," Freddie stated emphatically. "Calamity traveled up here in my private car at the rear of the train. We left it clear of the depot and went the back way to the Fair Lady. After we parted, I was kept talking at the back door for a few minutes. I could see the street all the time and nobody went along it."

"Even if they had trailed her to the hotel," drawled the Kid, "they'd still have to learn which room she was in."

"That'd be easy enough," Beauregard told him. "The register's always open on the reception desk and, after midnight, the clerk spends most of his time in the office. Calam's name'd be about the last in the book——"

"Only not as Calamity Jane," Freddie concluded. "And, as Charles said, not many people know her as Martha Jane Canary."

"So they could've found out which room I was in," Calamity said. "Why didn't they both come upstairs, 'stead of one of 'em trying to get in through the window?"

"To make doubly sure of reaching you," Freddie

guessed. "They couldn't be sure of being able to open the door——"

"And, like a blasted fool, I'd opened the window a mite," Calamity continued and, in self-exculpation, went on, "Whoever was there afore me used some fancy perfume that stunk like a cat-house comes a hot summer——"

"Nobody's blaming you for opening the window," Beauregard said gently. "But you did help them a mite by doing it."

"Ain't that *just* like a man, Freddie?" Calamity asked. " 'Nobody blames you, but——!' How was I to know they was after me? Do you reckon I sent up smoke-signals telling 'em I was coming?"

"I talk too much 'n' too loud when I've made a fool mistake," drawled the Kid. "Don't you, Kail, Counselor?"

"Mistake!" howled Calamity, rocketing to her feet like a startled bobwhite quail rising from a corn-patch. Then a spasm of pain contorted her features. "Damn it! Now you've started my hurts to aching again!"

"Sit down, Miss Canary," Talbot suggested, eyeing the Kid with disapproval. "Can I have my clerk fetch you a drink of water, or something?"

"Nope," the girl replied, dropping her rump to the chair. "They do say that cigar-smoke's right good for taking the hurt out of a sore jaw, though."

"It's a well-established non-medical fact," Freddie confirmed with a smile. "Go ahead, Charles. Smoke doesn't bother me."

Talbot let out an embarrassed sniff at the reminder of his lack of hospitality. Opening the cigar-box, he held it in Calamity's direction. If he expected the girl to be bluffing, he was rapidly proven wrong. Taking a cigar, Calamity twirled it appreciatively between her forefinger and thumb, bit off the end and accepted a light. Watching the girl for signs of distress as she sucked in the smoke, Talbot presented the box to the Kid and Beauregard.

"Now this here's what I call a good cigar," Calamity announced. "I can see why Lawyer Grosvenor didn't offer me a smoke. If I'd got cigars this good——"

"Who did you say?" Talbot interrupted.

"Grosvenor. That fancy law-wrangler down to Topeka's sent me to see you," Calamity replied. "Didn't he let you know I was coming?"

"No," Talbot stated. "I've not heard from him."

"Way you said that, Counselor," the Kid remarked, "I'd reckon you don't count this Grosvenor *hombre* what you'd call a honest, upstanding member of the Bar."

Before coming West, Talbot had believed its inhabitants were dull-witted, uneducated yokels. Since his arrival, he had discovered that many of them—despite lacking a formal education—could be remarkably shrewd and discerning. So he felt no surprise at the way the Kid had read the correct meaning to his words.

For his part, the Kid would receive the answer to his comment at first hand while handling the law in a corrupt town.* Beauregard appeared to know it already.

"He's so crooked, he leaves a trail like a sidewinder," the marshal declared.

"I wouldn't go that far," Talbot said cautiously.

"I would," Beauregard insisted. "He's kept more thieves and such out of the law's hands than I can count. All with legal trickery and pull in the State Legislature."

"That's never been proven——!" Talbot began, his instincts making him protect the reputation of a man he knew to be all the marshal had claimed.

"And is getting us away from the point," Freddie put in. "There could be several valid reasons why Grosvenor didn't inform Charles about Calamity coming. What we are trying to find out is how they knew where to find her, so that they could rob her of the papers that would prove her eligible for receiving the offer to buy the ranch. And don't ask me to repeat all that."

"It sounds to me like The Outfit's involved," Beauregard said gently.

"Which Outfit?" asked the Kid.

"I wished I knew," the marshal admitted. "It's

---

* Told in *The Small Texan* and *The Town Tamers*.

only rumors I've picked up, Kid, but there's a mighty well-organized bunch operating in and around Kansas. You want somebody killed, or got rid of, and've got the money to meet their prices, you go to The Outfit. They've fellers in every town, near on, and're said to use some of the Wells Fargo way station crews to pick up and pass on information."

"And you think they're involved?" Freddie inquired.

"Could be," Beauregard admitted. "I wouldn't put it past Grosvenor to be working for The Outfit."

"Then why send her all this way?" asked the Kid. "She could've been jumped and robbed just as easy in Topeka, especially if Grosvenor's mixed in the deal."

"Word has it that the State Legislature's getting interested in The Outfit," Beauregard answered. "So they wouldn't chance making a fuss that close to home."

"You think this 'Outfit' has men in Mulrooney, Marshal?" Talbot put in.

"I *know* it has, but not who they are. The Outfit's smart. They don't try to take over a town. They just keep a few hired guns around in case some're needed. Likely the fellers don't even know beyond whoever gives them pay in town."

"So Grosvenor sends Calam here and lets somebody know she's coming," the Kid said. "They wouldn't need to follow her to the hotel."

"They might, though," Freddie insisted. "If The Outfit pass information by telegraph, they would have to use a code, or make the messages sound harmless and nothing to do with what they really meant. That would mean they couldn't go into a lot of details or descriptions. So they would have had to keep a watch at the depot."

"If they had done, they'd've knowed she wasn't no shy lil Eastern gal," the Kid objected. "Least-ways, I've never seen any Eastern gal dressed like Calamity."

"What's wrong with how I dress?" Calamity bristled indignantly.

"Not a teensy thing from where I'm sitting," the Kid assured her. "Only I never saw no shy lil Eastern gal wearing pants, nor toting a Colt 'n' a bull-whip."

"Calamity didn't leave the train with the other passengers," Freddie announced. "So if they had a man watching, he wouldn't have seen her. Or didn't recognize her."

"You've maybe got it," drawled the Kid.

"Do you mean that The Outfit have been paid to scare Miss Calamity so that she would sell the ranch without wanting to visit it?" asked Talbot.

"Either that, or to steal the papers so that she couldn't prove her identity," Freddie agreed. "The answer is in Hollick City, unless you manage to catch the two men and make them talk, Kail."

"I'll do my damnedest on that," the marshal promised.

"And, unless you want for me to stick around, I'm headed for Hollick City just's soon's I can get me a good hoss," Calamity announced. "I don't take to fellers spoiling my sleep and whomping me across the jaw. So I'm headed up there to see why they've done it."

"You've got company, Calam gal, happen you want it," the Kid told her, coming to his feet. "Dusty told me to go back down to the herd, but he'll not mind if I don't when he hears why."

"Just hold on for a moment, you hotheads!" Freddie snapped as Calamity stood up. "You can have the pick of my stable, Calamity, and a pack-horse. But only if you show some sense. Lon, attend to your business with Charles. Kail, I dare say you've inquiries to make before you'll let Calamity leave. So I suggest that we break up this meeting and attend to our affairs."

Knowing that Freddie made real good sense, the others went along with her suggestions. Leaving the Kid with the lawyer, Calamity accompanied Freddie to the stable. Beauregard headed for his office to start his investigation.

Going to the telegraph office, after learning that the search for the two men had not yet produced any result, Beauregard was told that there had only been a couple of messages received from Topeka the previous day. One was from Grosvenor to the Railroad House Hotel, requesting that a room be reserved for Miss Martha Jane Canary. The other was to a general store, telling its owner that some supplies he had ordered were on their way. At any other time Beauregard might have ignored the second message. Remembering Freddie's comments about innocuous-appearing information, he decided to keep his eye on the store-keeper.

Leaving the telegraph office, the marshal almost walked into Calamity and the Kid. Freddie had insisted that they notify their respective employers of their intentions and they were on their way to do it. While telling them of his findings, Beauregard saw one of his deputies approaching.

"They got away, Kail," the man said miserably. "Feller allows he saw them riding out of town about half an hour after the shooting. They was headed north on the stage-trail."

"Which leads to Hollick City!" Beauregard growled. "They're taking your papers to whoever hired 'em up there, I'd say, Calamity."

"And me," the girl agreed. "Damn it! We can't get started afore noon to take after 'em."

"Was they riding relay, friend?" the Kid asked the deputy.

"Not according to the feller. Just the one hoss a-piece."

"Then we'll be traveling a whole heap faster'n they can, gal," the Kid declared. "Given just a smidgin of good Texas luck, we ought to catch up with 'em on the trail. Happen we do, we'll ask 'em real polite to give back that letter."

Chapter 6

THEY KNOW WE'RE AFTER 'EM

"How come I have to lead the pack-hoss?" Calamity Jane inquired belligerently as she and the Kid rode north along the stagecoach trail.

" 'Cause you're a woman," her companion replied. "And us *Pehnane* fellers allus keep our women in their place."

"I ain't no blasted *Pehnane*, no matter what you might be!" the girl protested. "So we'll take us turns in leading this fool critter."

Adding the pack-horse to the two reserve mounts she had borrowed from Freddie did not cause Calamity any inconvenience. In fact she had led it ever since they had mounted their relays in Mulrooney at noon and the sun was dipping toward the western horizon. However, she felt that she ought to have certain matters straightened out. From what Mark Counter had told her, the Kid rated women above a food-dog but lower than a pack-mule on the scale of importance. So the girl had decided that it was up to her to raise the standing of females in her companion's eyes and make him change such fool notions.

Before leaving the town, Beauregard had told them of his latest findings; which had not been much. Smith had been seen around the depot the previous night and on two occasions in the company of two men answering the descriptions of Calamity's assailants. On being questioned, the day clerk at the Railroad House Hotel had insisted that he knew nothing of Smith's presence across the street when Calamity had left to visit Talbot. Beauregard believed that the man was lying. Beyond that, there was nothing definite. The whole affair had still struck the marshal as being the work of The Outfit. His view was strengthened by the speed with which the pair had left the town. After losing one man, the organizer for The Outfit would speed the others involved on their way without any delay as they had completed their work.

Thinking of Beauregard's comments, the Kid saw what might be a solution to Calamity's demands.

"Way I see it," he remarked, "with them two

pelados on the trail ahead and all, you should lead the pack-hoss and leave me free should it come to shooting."

"If it comes to shooting, I don't want tying down to no blasted pack-hoss neither," Calamity countered. "So, comes morning, we take turns in leading it."

"Banged paleface!" grunted the Kid.

"*Pehnane* varmint," the girl answered.

Watching Calamity, the Kid was satisfied with what he saw. He knew the girl to be highly competent at handling a six-horse wagon, but riding relay was a different proposition. From all he had seen so far, she possessed the necessary riding skill to stand up to the fast pace they must use if they hoped to catch the two men. There was another matter for the Kid to consider.

"Does Mark mean anything to you, Calam?" he asked.

"I wish he did," she sighed. "There's only one gal in his life and her name's Belle Starr, not Calamity Jane."*

Topping a rim at that moment, they came into sight of Wells Fargo's North Solomon River way station. That prevented Calamity from taking the matter any further, although she guessed what was on the Kid's mind.

---

* How the romance between Belle Starr and Mark Counter ended is told in *Guns in the Night*.

The way station would have been a day's journey by stagecoach, but the vehicle would have left Mulrooney shortly after sunup and traveled more slowly than Calamity's and the Kid's relays. Halting his horses, the Kid studied the deserted aspect of the main building, big barn and corrals.

"They could be laying for us in the house or the barn," Calamity remarked, having duplicated his scrutiny. "Best give me the reins of your relay, Lon. Only don't count on me leading them all the way to Hollick City."

"Us *Pehnane* don't trust the women-folk to lead our *riding*-hosses most times," he replied, handing her the reins of the three horses.

With Calamity spluttering a blanket condemnation of the *Pehnane,* Texans and himself, the Kid slid his rifle from its saddle-boot. Then he started the magnificent seventeen-hand white stallion moving. Calamity let him draw slightly ahead before following with the other horses.

"You bunch cause me fuss, comes shooting," the girl warned the animals, "and I'll peel you to doll-rags with my whip, see if I don't."

While approaching the long, one-story, stone building that acted as telegraph office, hotel, saloon and general store, Calamity and the Kid kept constantly alert. They had come to within thirty yards of the building before they saw anything to alarm them. Then the door started to open and they observed the twin barrels of a shotgun coming into view.

Instantly the Kid halted his stallion, the rifle lifting slightly from its place across his upper thighs. Behind him, Calamity brought the other horses to a stop. Her right hand moved toward the butt of the Navy Colt, but she knew that her main task in the event of shooting would be to control the animals.

The shotgun's barrels retreated into the building and after a moment a man walked out. While tall, his lean build, white hair, bib-overalls and moccasins proved that he was not one of Calamity's attackers. Coming to a halt on the edge of the porch, he thumb-hooked his hands into his belt. It appeared that he trusted the new arrivals, for he no longer held the shotgun—assuming that it had been him who had allowed it to show.

"Howdy," greeted the Kid, slouching apparently at ease but ready to burst into sudden, violent motion should the need arise.

Slowly the old man shifted a wad of tobacco into his left cheek and cut loose with a spurt of juice. His eyes took in every detail of the newcomers' appearance, resting for a moment on the rifle held with such deceptive negligence in the Kid's hands.

"Light 'n' rest your saddles," the man offered.

"*Gracias,*" drawled the Kid, dismounting without looking at Calamity. "Can we bed the hosses down in the stable tonight?"

"Feel free," the old-timer answered. "It's empty right now."

"Nobody staying with you?" Calamity asked.

"Nope. Was you expecting somebody?"

Remembering what Beauregard had said about The Outfit making use of Wells Fargo employees—without the Company's knowledge or consent—as gatherers of information and message-carriers, the Kid decided against taking chances.

"Can't say 'yes' to that," he answered, giving Calamity no time to speak. "Not 'less it's the gal's pappy. He don't cotton to having me for a son-in-law."

"There's some'd say the feller'd right good taste," the old-timer sniffed and turned his attention to the girl. "Only I never knowed you'd got a pappy, Calam."

"You figure maybe I was left under the blueberry bushes by the fairies, you wored-out ole goat?" Calamity demanded, walking forward. "Lon, meet Deke Goff. Not that he's worth meeting. Deke, this here's the Ysabel Kid, and I'm right ashamed to be seed in his company."

"Why in hell didn't you say you knowed the gent?" growled the Kid, after booting his rifle and shaking hands with the grinning old man.

"I just naturally loves to see a smart yahoo like you make a fool of hisself is why," Calamity answered. "As if a sweet-looking, lovable gal like me'd marry up with a mean, ornery *Pehnane* varmint like you."

"I might've been took in, Kid," Goff commented. "Only I mind you from when you was a deputy in Mulrooney. So I reckoned anybody Cap'n Fog'd pin a tin star on'd be too smart to marry a freight-hauling she-male with a temp——"

"Damned if you men don't all hang together!" Calamity yelped. "And should. There's not one of you to improve on the rest. Come on, hosses, let's leave 'em."

Leading the way to the open doors of the barn, Goff looked over his shoulder and said, "Way you pair rid up, Kid, I'd say you was expecting somebody."

"Two of 'em," the Kid confirmed, knowing now that he could trust the old man. So he described Calamity's attackers for Goff's benefit.

"Does the Mex ride a fancy light red roan, with a white belly?" asked the old man. "What they call *sabino,* or some such."

"That's what they call 'em," agreed the Kid. "Only we don't know what sort of hosses him and his pard's riding. Have they been through here today?"

"T'other feller's riding a light bay with a white blaze down its face and a white off fore-leg," Goff remarked, stepping aside inside the barn and indicating the empty stalls. "Take any you want. Come by maybe ten days back, headed for Mulrooney. The Mex had a misplaced eyebrow then, but not when he come back this afternoon, going north again. Would there be some special reason you're asking about 'em?"

"They jumped me in town this morning and wide-looped a letter I was carrying," Calamity informed him.

"Must've been a mighty important letter for 'em to tangle with you pair to get it," Goff commented.

"I wasn't with her when it happened," the Kid explained. "How long is it since they went by?"

"Maybe three, four hours. They stopped off for a meal and lit out soon's I'd fed 'em. Mex was walking kinda stiff, like he'd got him a sore crotch."

"I was hoping he'd have one," Calamity enthused, delighted that one of her attackers still felt the effects of her efforts. " 'Cause I sure tried to get him that way."

"Being a gent born 'n' raised, I ain't going to ask what that means," Goff stated. "I thought they was watching their back trail kind of careful. The rest of the boys being in Mulrooney for the day, I didn't ask 'em about it. Tell you one thing, was you to ask."

"We're asking," Calamity sighed, looking at the roof as if searching for divine assistance.

"They'll not be traveling too fast."

"How come?" asked the Kid.

"The big feller's hoss looked ready to throw a shoe," Goff explained. "Can't get it fixed afore he reaches the way station at the joining of the Sappa 'n' Beaver Creeks over in Nebrasky. And I'd be tolerable surprised if it got him that far."

All the time they had been talking, the old-timer was helping Calamity and the Kid to place their horses in the stalls and attend to the animals' needs. Going on with the work, he confirmed that the big man's name was "Job," while the Mexican answered to "Otón," although no surnames had been used.

"Unsociable pair," Goff grunted. "Reckon you can finish off while I go tend to supper?"

"We'll try," promised the Kid.

"What'll we do about them?" Calamity inquired as Goff left the barn.

"Do you reckon we should've kept on's soon's we heard they'd been here?"

"Nope. It'll be dark soon, long afore we could catch up with 'em anyways. And I don't figure they'll make camp where we could easy find 'em."

"I never knowed you used your head 'cept as a place to hang that beat-up blue-belly's hat on," the Kid told her admiringly.

"You want for me to tell you what I've allus heard about you?" Calamity asked.

"Couldn't be anything but goodness, so go to it."

They had finished with their last horse and stood face-to-face outside the stalls. Watching

Calamity suck in a deep breath ready to blast him with profanity, the Kid grinned. No matter how their journey to Hollick turned out, he was in mighty stimulating company to make it.

"Anyways," the Kid went on, giving her no time to launch her tirade, "I reckon we should spend the night here and move on with the hosses rested comes morning. What Deke told us, they figure on being followed. I'd say that that Otón *hombre* for one'd have some smart notions about how to stop whoever's doing the following."

"Do you know him?"

"Can't say I do. I didn't see him close enough up for that. But I know his kind, Calam gal. They're tricky, hawg-mean and deadly as a stick-teased diamondback."

Listening to the quietly spoken words, Calamity put aside her intention of pouring invective on the Kid's head. The warning had been given by a man who knew full well what he was talking about. So she realized just how dangerous the journey to Hollick might turn out.

Satisfied that their horses wanted for nothing, Calamity and the Kid left the stable. They had placed their saddles on the inverted V-shaped wooden "burro" supplied for that purpose, but took their Winchesters with them. Going across to the big house, they entered to find its center front room deserted. After a moment, Goff appeared through the door leading into the telegraph office.

"You'll have to wait supper a mite," the old-timer remarked. "There was a message started coming through just after I'd gotten into the kitchen. I missed the call sign, but reckoned I'd best take it down case it was for me. What I got was 'White stallion and red mare on their way to your ranch.' There didn't seem to be no signature."

"Any notion where it'd come from and where it was going?" asked the Kid.

"It'd come up from Mulrooney, but might've been passed from beyond that. If it warn't for here, which I doubt seeing's this ain't ranching country, it could be for any of the way stations between here 'n' Hollick City, or out beyond that. We get messages telling folks to come 'n' collect something, or something's coming, going through all the time."

"Sure," agreed the Kid. "Only it could be about us. I don't know if that Mexican recognized me. But if he did, he'd likely recall that I ride a white stallion."

"Only we don't have a red mare," Calamity pointed out.

"I called 'n' asked Mulrooney where that message'd been sent," Goff put in. "It was for the Sappa 'n' Beaver Creek way station."

"What's the fellers who run it like?"

"Well, I'll tell you, Kid. My mammy raised me proper that if I couldn't say nothing nice about folks, not to talk about 'em. You got another question?"

"Not right now," the Kid admitted, for the other's reticence had told him all he needed to know.

"I'll go finish supper, then," Goff decided and ambled away.

"What do you reckon, Lon?" Calamity inquired as the old-timer went through a door leading to the rear of the building.

"There's two ways of looking at it," the Kid replied gravely. "Either it was to a rancher telling him two hosses he's ordered're coming. Or somebody from The Outfit's passing word to Otón 'n' Job. If it's the first, it's harmless. But if it's the second, they know we're after them. Or will when they hit that way station."

"Yeah," Calamity breathed.

"How well do you know Deke?"

"Well enough to trust him."

"That's good enough for me. Anyways, if it'd been for him to pass on, he'd not've mentioned it."

"What do we do about it?" asked Calamity.

"Can't do a thing today," the Kid pointed out. "They won't get the message until so late tonight, or early tomorrow, that they'd not be able to get back here afore day-break. So we'll have us some supper, then grab some sleep."

"Is that *all* we'll do tonight?" the girl inquired innocently.

"Can't think of anything else," answered the Kid. "Except we'll ride *real* careful from now on."

"Know something?" Calamity sniffed. "I'm beginning to think Mark had a mishap and told me the truth about you."

She turned and walked over to sit at one of the tables without elaborating on which aspect of Mark Counter's information about the Kid she had meant. Joining her, the dark young Texan settled on a chair and they waited for their supper in silence.

"Dang it!" Deke announced as he served their meal. "I just thought. The boys done took all the bedding into Mulrooney to get it washed, 'cepting for one bed's, seeing's there warn't no stage due tonight."

"I can bunk down in the barn," offered the Kid.

"Or we could 'bundle,' Lon," Calamity suggested, eyeing him in a challenging manner. "There's no harm in it."

"No harm at all," agreed Deke, "when it's done proper."

"Bundling" had come into being during the early days of the country's colonization. The settlers soon discovered that the winter nights were long and bitterly cold. So they had been forced to revise their conventions for courting couples. When a young man had traveled many miles to visit his sweetheart, they wanted privacy. Sitting out on the porch did not offer an answer in winter. Nor could the thrifty settlers contemplate the expense of heating and illuminating a separate room for the couple's use. So they had been allowed to "bundle," share a bed, with a pine-board between them to preserve their virtue. That did away with the need for artificial heating, as they could lie side by side in the darkness and the bed's clothes would keep them warm.

When the migration to the West had begun, the travelers found "bundling" answered their needs and it grew into a frontier institution.

"We'll do that, then," the Kid declared.

After supper, Calamity went into the room indicated by Goff. As he always did, even when at the OD Connected ranch-house, the Kid paid a final visit to the barn and checked on his horses. Returning to the station building, he found that Goff had already retired. When he entered the bedroom, he saw Calamity had started to undress. Her boots and socks lay by the foot of the bed. Draped across the seat of a chair were her jacket, shirt and undershirt. Looking across her shoulder, she allowed her trousers to slide down.

"What're you doing?" the Kid asked, unbuckling his gunbelt and hanging it with Calamity's on the hook behind the door.

"My mammy allus taught me not to sleep in my street clothes," the girl replied. "You wouldn't want me to go against her word, now would you?"

"That wouldn't be right," the Kid admitted, tossing his hat by her kepi on the small dressing-table. " 'Fact my pappy allus used to tell me the same thing."

Blowing out the lamp, the Kid undressed and joined Calamity in the bed. For a time they lay on their backs, then he felt the girl's inner hand feeling at the blanket between them.

"What's up?" he asked.

"Danged if we haven't forgotten to get a pineboard to put between us," Calamity replied and turned on to her side. "What're we going to do about it?"

With the first streak of dawn creeping in the eastern sky, Calamity watched the Kid don a breechclout of Comanche blue. Swinging her legs from the bed, she studied his lean, steel-wire muscled, hard frame. Giving a slight shiver, she grabbed her undershirt from the chair. Wriggling into it, she gathered in her shirt, drawers and trousers.

"You'd best put a shirt on," Calamity remarked as the Kid went to the door clad only to his waist, including his gunbelt.

"I'm fixing to," he replied and left the room.

On his return, he wore a light gray shirt and multi-colored bandana. Calamity had already completed dressing and eyed him with interest.

"Why the change?" she asked.

"Happen that feller, Otón, sees me now," the Kid explained, "he could figure he was wrong and

I'm not the Ysabel Kid. That happens, he'll be a mite easier to handle."

"What would you've done last night if there'd been anything between Mark 'n' me?" Calamity said, picking up her carbine which she had brought, along with the Kid's rifle, into the room the previous evening.

"Slept in the barn," the Kid answered. "Fact being, if there was anything between you 'n' old Mark, I'd've had no other choice."

"You know something, Lon," Calamity said seriously. "That's just about the nicest thing anybody's ever said to me." Then a merry glint came to her eyes. "Hey though. I've showed you a gal can do one thing better'n any old food-dog or pack-mule."

Chapter 7

THAT WHITE STALLION AND RED MARE

AT FIRST SIGHT, THE WAY STATION ON THE SOUTHERN bank of the river formed by the joining of the Beaver and Sappa Creeks looked much like the place in which Calamity and the Kid had spent the previous night. Going closer, they noticed that it lacked the tidiness and well-kept appearance of Deke Goff's establishment. None of the staff, four in number according to Goff, were working outside the buildings. Smoke curled up from the chimney of the blacksmith's forge between the main buildings, corrals and the river. The trail went through the station property and crossed a ford to continue its passage north.

Once again Calamity led all the horses, complaining bitterly about it, despite the suggestion that she should having come from her. Searching the buildings with careful gaze, they felt that they had one advantage over their arrival at Goff's place. Now they knew what kind of horses Otón and Job rode. Maybe the bay could go unnoticed among the other animals in the corrals, but Otón's *sabino* ought to be distinctive enough to be picked out. An examination of the corrals did not produce a reddish-roan horse with a white belly. However, it could be concealed in the barn.

"We'll play it like that's where they've got their hosses," the Kid drawled. "Only we'll make out we don't suspect anything."

"They'd've had to stop off here if that hoss' shoe we found back on the trail come from Job's bay," Calamity replied. "Looks like the forge's been used today."

Because of their precautions, they reached the buildings without being fired on or challenged. Before they had left that morning, Goff had gone against his mother's advice and told them enough about the crew of the way station to make them wary. So they had eaten a meal on the trail shortly after noon and pushed on another two hours to their present location. It was their intention to water the horses and ride on, unless Otón and Job were at the way station and disputed their passing.

"Take all the hosses, Calam," the Kid ordered,

dropping from his saddle. "I want to nose around a mite."

"You're starting to talk like a Comanche again," the girl warned, but rode by the forge on her way to obey.

The Kid did not intend to do his "nosing around" in the station's main building or barn, which they had already passed. Dropping from his saddle, he removed the stallion's bridle and bit. Hanging them across the low-horned, double-girthed Texas saddle, he allowed the white to follow the other horses. Then he turned his attention to the forge. It had been constructed on spartan lines. Apart from the roof's supports, three sides were open. The forth had a wall, but merely as backing for the furnace's chimney.

Going through the open side nearest him, the Kid looked around. The forge showed the same lax, unkempt state as the rest of the station. Bits of iron, broken farm implements, a pick-handle that had lost its head and other oddments lay in a sizeable untidy heap, discarded or tossed aside to be used at some later date. A turning-hammer lay on the anvil, instead of among the other neglected-looking tools hanging on the wall. It was not a place to inspire confidence if one had a horse that needed shoeing. However, everything intimated that work had been done in it recently. Not in the last two or three hours, maybe, but certainly since sunup.

Hearing footsteps approaching from the other buildings, the Kid turned slowly. He made no gesture that could be construed as hostile, but was ready to take instant, effective action should the sounds be produced by the two men from Mulrooney.

Facing the new arrivals, the Kid saw that they were not Job and Otón. In fact three, not two, men came toward him. Thinking back to what Goff had told him, the Kid identified the trio.

The big, gaunt, dirty-looking cuss at the right of the group, showing off brawny biceps in a sleeveless undershirt, with grimy pants and heavy boots, would be Tully, the blacksmith. In the center, medium height, stocky, wearing range clothes, a scar half-hidden by whiskers on his right cheek, was the wrangler, Masters. Gangling, mournful, living up to his name "Misery," the last of them combined wrangling and cooking. He must have put more than one traveler off his food.

That left the station agent to be accounted for. According to Deke Goff, Marty Spatz did as little manual work as he could manage. So the "duded-up, city-dressed bladder of rancid lard," to quote the old-timer's description, would most likely be in one of the buildings and watching what his hired help figured on doing.

Despite the fact that none of them wore a gun, they aimed to do something, or the Kid missed his guess. Their whole attitude hinted at that. Walking under the roof of the forge, Tully and Masters confronted the Kid. Acting just a mite too casual, Misery sauntered by the building. Darting a glance after the lean man, the Kid saw that he was making toward where Calamity stood watching the horses drinking.

"Want something?" Tully demanded.

"One of the hosses there throwed a shoe," the Kid replied, wondering if he should warn the girl. "I was fixing to get it tended to after they'd watered."

"Wasn't fixing on tending to it yourself, was you?" Tully growled.

"Why?" countered the Kid. "Ain't there a blacksmith here?"

Standing on slightly parted feet, the Kid looked very young and inexperienced. The changing out of his black shirt seemed to add to his youth. It was, however, an attitude that would have fooled nobody who knew him. Tully and Masters lacked that advantage. To them, the Kid was a bald-faced stripling who figured to be one real savage curlywolf. He ought to be easy enough meat for what they had been sent to do. Not that they aimed to take chances. Having formed a different opinion at the sight of him passing from a distance, they had not worn their guns. That old Dragoon had seen some use and a bowie knife could be as deadly when slashed wildly by a scared kid, as it would be in the hands of a man skilled in its use.

"Folks's want the blacksmith most times stop at the house and ask for him," Tully stated, exuding a menace that ought to hold the Texan's attention while Masters sidled past him. "Them's don't ain't up to any good, way I see it. There's a heap of valuable gear here, most of it light enough to be toted off on a hoss."

"And that's what you reckon I was fixing to do, huh?" the Kid inquired, with a mildness that would have screamed a warning to anybody aware of his ways.

Even as he spoke, a faint clatter from one side and slightly behind him reached his ears. He knew that the sound had originated from inside the building and not down by the stream. Nor did he need to turn to guess at its cause. Confident that his actions were unsuspected, Masters was picking up a weapon. Thinking of what he had seen on his arrival, the Kid decided that it would most likely be the pick-handle. Nothing else in the heap of rubbish would be light or handy enough to serve the stocky man's purpose. However, the Indian-dark young Texan showed no hint of being aware of what went on behind his back.

"I ain't saying you was, and I ain't saying you wasn't," the blacksmith declared, devoting most of his attention to where Misery was drawing closer to the apparently unsuspecting girl. "Only, seeing's how I wore blue in the War, I don't cotton to Texas beef-heads coming here and making free with my property."

"Maybe I've come to pick up that white stallion and red mare that're on the way from Mulrooney," the Kid suggested and saw surprise twist at Tully's face, to be replaced by anger and a little alarm.

Gripping the thin end of the pick-handle in both hands, Masters crept toward the Kid. The wrangler could not hold down a hiss of surprise when he realized what the young Texan had said. Then he swung the handle around, like a baseball player wielding the bat, aiming to drive its splintered, swollen head between the shoulders of the gray shirt. Struck there with paralyzing force, the cowhand would be unable to resist the rest of what they had been ordered out to do.

Satisfied that his companions could chill the male visitor's milk without requiring help from him, Misery ignored what was going on in the forge. To him had been assigned the more enjoyable, and maybe safer, task of subduing the girl. Which ought to be easy enough, no matter how she dressed. He could see the bottom of the Colt's holster, which did not greatly alarm him, but the bull-whip was concealed by her buckskin jacket. She still continued to stand with her back to him, gazing across the river and oblivious of her peril.

Unfortunately for him, Calamity was nowhere near so unsuspecting as Misery fondly imagined.

Having seen the trio making for the forge, she had expected trouble. When Misery left his companions, she figured that she had called the play correctly. She also decided that the Kid might need help and reckoned that she could supply it, after she had handed her mournful-featured assailant the shock of his life.

Having turned her head to the front before any of the trio became aware that she had seen them, Calamity listened to Misery's footsteps approaching. Undetected by the lanky man, she slipped the whip's handle from its belt loop and loosened the lash ready for use.

"If I'm doing you wrong, I'll say 'sorry' most humble," Calamity thought. "If I ain't, you're asking for all you're going to get, you scrawny, miserable-looking son-of-a-bitch."

With that, Calamity started to pivot around in Misery's direction. One glance told her that she had gauged the sound of his feet correctly. He was within range of her whip. Shock twisted at Misery's face as he realized that he had been detected. Before he could decide on what action to take, Calamity made her move.

On the off-chance that the men might not have evil intentions, Calamity had decided not to make the whip perform at its most lethal potential. Using her turning momentum to extend the long lash, she swung her right arm sideways, to the rear and snapped it forward. Almost as if it possessed a will of its own, the lash followed the movement. It curled through the air parallel to the ground in the direction of the lean man. Hard-plaited leather wrapped around Misery's forward ankle while the foot was still in the air. Even through his boot, he felt the crushing pressure of its hold.

Bracing her feet, Calamity gave a jerk on the whip. She caused Misery to hop on his other foot in an attempt to keep his balance. Darting toward him, she slid her hand to the upper end of the handle. As she came into range, before the man had recovered his equilibrium, she crashed the loaded butt of the handle against the side of his jaw. The force of the blow snapped his head sideways and he collapsed as if he had been pole-axed. Calamity threw a look at the forge, from which the sounds of strife had warned that her suspicions were correct. What she saw caused her to drop the whip, spin around and race toward the horses.

Hearing the sound of Masters approaching from the rear, the Kid prepared to meet the danger. He had not heard any disturbance from Calamity's direction, but hoped the girl could take care of herself until he could give her some help. In turning to meet his attacker, the Kid thrust his right leg to the rear and bent his left knee. At the same time, he bowed his torso forward and crouched with such speed that he took Masters by surprise.

Despite seeing his proposed victim's movements, the wrangler could not halt his attack. The pick-handle swung around and whistled above the Kid's head. Driving himself forward with the abrupt, instantaneous impetus shown by a cougar making an attack, the Texan locked his arms around the top of Masters' thighs. Straightening up, the Kid raised the unbalanced, amazed man from the ground and heaved him over. The moment he released Masters, the Kid lunged forward and started to swing around.

In falling, Masters rammed his head against the floor of the forge, and the hard-packed earth came off better from the encounter. The wrangler crumpled and landed almost at the feet of the charging blacksmith. Distracted by the sight of Calamity effectively coping with Misery, Tully belatedly tried to leap over his companion. Instead, his forward foot caught against Masters' body and he stumbled as he landed. Big hands reaching for a hold, the blacksmith blundered toward the Kid. Jumping aside, the Kid caused the hands to miss. As Tully went by, the Kid drove a kick into his rump, which increased his speed.

During his evasion of Tully's attack, the Kid had approached the anvil. Tully continued across the forge at a fast clip, but managed to hook his left arm around one of the roof's support-posts. Using it to turn him, he started to charge again. The Kid wanted to end the matter swiftly, in case Calamity needed his assistance. Nearby lay the means by which he could do so. Scooping up the turning

hammer from the anvil, he was reminded of
Pehnane war-clubs he had seen and handled as a
boy. Like a flash, he hurled the hammer as he had
been taught by Grandpappy Long Walker. Flying
across the forge, its head struck Tully between the
eyes. Halted in his tracks, the blacksmith buckled
at the knees and sprawled face down on the floor.

With the hammer thrown and its results observed, the Kid swiftly looked around. Tully no
longer posed any threat and Masters lay where he
had fallen. About to swing toward the river, a
movement caught the corner of the Kid's eye.
Turning his head, he saw a portly, bald man running from the rear door of the main building.
Wearing a collarless shirt, fancy vest, town suit and
boots, he fit the description Goff had given of
Agent Spatz. Which interested the Kid far less than
the fact that the newcomer carried a double-
barreled shotgun. Finding his presence had been
detected, Spatz skidded to a halt and began to raise
the weapon.

Right hand turning palm-out and fanging down
to close about the Dragoon's butt, the Kid vaulted
over the anvil. It would not be large enough to
offer him shelter from the shotgun's spreading pat-
tern of balls. Ahead was the pile of rubbish from
which the pick-handle had come. It was of sufficient size and quality to give him protection—if he
could reach it in time. At that range, Spatz would
be unlikely to miss with a charge of buckshot. The

chance had to be taken. To stay put would mean almost certain death. Bringing the Dragoon from leather, the Kid threw himself across the open space between the anvil and the pile of rubbish.

Calamity had also seen Spatz appear and knew that she could not handle the situation with her whip. Letting it fall, she darted to the horses and snatched her Winchester carbine from its saddle-boot. Swiveling around, she advanced three strides. Then she knew that she must stop moving and start shooting. Dropping her right knee to the ground, she adopted a firing position as fast as she had ever made it. Taking sight, she squeezed the trigger.

With his shotgun starting to line on the Kid, Spatz found the arrival of Calamity's bullet very disconcerting. Dirt erupted between his feet, causing him to jerk hurriedly backward and press both triggers of his weapon. Bellowing like a cannon, the twin tubes discharged their loads. They had lifted when their user made his involuntary retreat, so the eighteen buckshot balls plowed into the roof of the forge. In his surprise, Spatz had relaxed his grip on the gun. So the recoil hurled the butt against his shoulder with numbing force. Letting out a screech of pain, he released and dropped the weapon.

Landing belly-down behind the heap of rubbish, the Kid heard the whip-like crack of Calamity's carbine mingle with the boom from the shotgun and the buckshot's impact on the roof over his head. Raising himself until he could see over the cover, he slanted the Dragoon in Spatz's direction.

The agent stood with an expression of pain and shock on his face. It changed to raw fear as he turned his head and located Calamity. Already the girl's right hand had returned the loading lever to its closed position. As his eyes focused on her, she laid her sights at his expansive stomach with cold deliberation.

"Make a move and you're dead!" Calamity yelled.

"If she don't get you, I will," promised the Kid.

Finding himself covered by two weapons in obviously capable hands, and with his full working staff sprawled unconscious on the ground, Spatz knew there could be only one course left open to him. Surrender and hope to talk himself out of the reprisals his would-be victims might be considering taking against him.

Sick anxiety filled the agent as he massaged his numb, aching right shoulder. On learning what he had wanted them to do, his men had stated that they would not go up against that alert, proddy-looking Texan with guns. So Spatz had persuaded them that they could take the visitors with their bare hands. In fact, he had told them, their victims would be less likely to expect trouble from un-armed men.

Studying the cold, Comanche-mean features of

the Ysabel Kid as he rose from behind the rubbish heap, Spatz felt his anxiety increase rapidly. The agent began to wish that he had never listened to the suggestions of his previous pair of visitors, or taken their money to prevent the girl and the Texan following them.

Deciding that the Kid could deal with the agent, Calamity came to her feet. She looked at the horses, wanting to make sure that they had not been disturbed by the shooting. Satisfied on that score, she tucked the carbine on the crook of her right arm and walked to where Misery lay. Removing her whip from his ankle, she strolled toward the forge, coiling its lash.

"You all right, Lon?" she asked, returning the handle to its belt loop.

"Well enough," the Kid replied, joining her. "You?"

"He never come close. What's it all about, Lon?"

"We've got the feller here's can tell us," the Kid answered, nodding to Spatz. "The lady asked a polite question, *hombre*. Why'd your hired help jump us?"

"This here's the Ysabel Kid, fatso," Calamity warned. "He don't look it, but he's got him a real mean temper when he's lied to."

Spatz might have disputed the statement about how the Kid looked. Instead he stared at the

Indian-dark Texan and croaked, "The Ysabel Kid?"

"That's me," the Kid admitted. "And, seeing's how we're getting so all-fired friendly, this's Calamity Jane. I bet Otón 'n' Job never told you who we was."

"They sure as hell didn't!" Spatz agreed indignantly.

"Then what'd they tell you to make you try 'n' jump us?" Calamity demanded.

"My men're hur——!" Spatz began.

The words ended abruptly as the Kid's left hand laid hold of their speaker's shirt-front and hauled him forward. The Dragoon's muzzle bored hard into Spatz's belly and a savage face came close to the agent's perspiring, frightened features.

"They won't be the only ones that way," warned the Kid, "happen I don't real quick get some answers."

"Hey! Easy there, Kid!" Spatz yelped placatingly as the Texan thrust him away. "Them two fellers come here. Allowed they'd been to Mulrooney and the greaser'd killed a feller who was trying to pull the badger game on him. Reckoned the dead feller's gal 'n' brother was gunning for 'em."

"And you thought we was them?" Calamity finished for him.

"I didn't know. That's what I sent the boys out to ask. Only I ought to've remembered——"

"About what?" prompted the Kid, holstering his Colt.

"I ought to've thought. Tully don't cotton to Texans. Anyways, when I saw them jump you, I come right out to stop them."

"I just bet you did," drawled the Kid. "Who were those two fellers?"

"I've never seen 'em afore," Spatz replied.

"Not even in Hollick City?" asked the Kid.

"I don't often go up there. Mulrooney's a whole heap livelier."

"How about that telegraph message they got?"

"Hey!" Spatz ejaculated. "It was right after I give it to 'em that they told me about the trouble in Mulrooney. They must've knowed you was coming, Kid, and slickered me into helping 'em."

"Why sure!" snorted Calamity. "I'll just bet that's what they did."

"And me," the Kid agreed mildly. "Only I'm wondering if ole Jim Hume'll see it that way."

"Ji——!" Spatz gasped. "You know Mr. Hume?"

"Well enough," the Kid replied. "I'm a deputy, special hired by the folks of Mulrooney, so I'm wanting help from you, *hombre*."

Spatz gulped, knowing how long he would continue to hold his lucrative position after Wells Fargo's head trouble-shooter heard of his activities. Even if the Kid was not so well-acquainted as he claimed with Jim Hume, the mayor of Mulrooney knew him. Freddie Woods was noted for the backing she gave to her town's peace officers. The agent decided that cooperation was his only hope of remaining in employment. So he forced a friendly smile.

"What do you want to know, Kid?"

"When'd they pull out?"

"Be just after noon, I'd say. Right after Tully'd fitted a new shoe on the white feller's hoss."

"Do they work for The Outfit?"

"Not any mo—— I don't know what outfit you mean, Kid."

"Let's go, Calam," the Kid growled, sensing that he would learn nothing more from the man.

"Er—Kid," Spatz said. "I was going to stop them——"

"Sure you was," the Kid replied. "And I won't say nothing about it to Jim—— Happen you don't telegraph ahead about that white stallion and red mare coming. I'm not partial to being talked about that way."

"Or me!" Calamity yelped, realizing what the Kid meant. "Red mare!"

"I wouldn't do that, Kid!" Spatz whined. "You can count on it."

Turning their backs on the frightened agent, Calamity and the Kid went by the forge to collect their horses. Neither of them looked around as they rode across the ford. On dry ground once more, the girl let out a snort of disgust.

"Do you reckon that they spun him a windy like he told us?" she asked. "And he believed it?"

"Nope. He thought it up real quick as an excuse for what his bunch'd tried to do."

"And we're going to let him get away with it that easy?"

"You want for me to go back 'n' scalp him, ears 'n' all?" grinned the Kid. " 'Cause apart from that, or burning down the station comes night-fall—which Jim Hume'd reckon was damage to Company property—there ain't a whole heap's we can do."

Giving her companion a cold glare that bounced right off him, Calamity scanned the range ahead.

"They've got about a three-hour start on us, Lon. Like you said, we're making better time than they are."

"Sure enough are, gal."

"And one of 'em's likely got my letter."

"Likely," agreed the Kid, glancing up at the sky. "Only we'll not catch up with 'em today. Won't've reached another way station before dark, neither."

"So I've used the ground for a mattress and the sky for a roof afore now."

"I ain't gainsaying it. Only when we make camp, it'll be without a fire. Just in case them two *pela-dos* figure Spatz's bunch didn't stop us and come back to do it personal."

"Would having 'em come back looking for us be so bad?" Calamity asked.

"Not's long's we knowed they was likely to do it," admitted the Kid. "Which's why I reckon we shouldn't take chances tonight."

"You're the boss," Calamity conceded.

"Then why'm I leading the pack-hoss?" asked the Kid.

.

Chapter 8

WE'LL TAKE THEM WHILE THEY SLEEP

∽⌇∾

Otón Ruiz felt uneasy as he rode with Job Hogue into the woods beyond the Silvers' way station on the Platte River. Turning in his saddle, he looked back at the buildings.

"*Hijo de puta!*" the Mexican spat out, reining his *sabino* around.

Wondering what had disturbed his companion, Hogue swung his bay to face in the direction from which they had come. He stared back across the half a mile that separated them from the buildings. At first he could detect nothing to have brought about the other man's actions. Then he looked beyond the way station and felt relieved by the fact that the trees and undergrowth flanking the trail hid them from the buildings and the ford behind them. Letting out an Anglo-Saxon curse even viler than his companion's Spanish comment, Hogue turned his eyes to the other's face. Ruiz was grinning in a faintly mocking manner.

"It appears that your *amigo* Spatz failed to do what he promised and was paid well for," the Mexican said dryly.

"Yeah!" Hogue answered. "And the lard-gutted son-of-a-bitch never even telegraphed to let us know they'd got by his men." Turning his gaze back to the two riders crossing the ford, each leading three horses, he reached for his rifle. "Looks like we'll have to tend to their needings ourselves."

Deciding that repeating the reminder that it had been Hogue's idea to hire Spatz would get them nowhere, Ruiz scowled at the way station. Clearly the attempt had been a failure, which was very annoying. All the previous afternoon they had watched their back trail without seeing a sign of their pursuers. Despite Hogue's belief that all had gone as planned, Ruiz had insisted on finding a high point when the sun went down. From it they had scoured the land behind them, searching for a sight of a camp-fire to tell them that the girl and her companion were still following on their trail. They had seen nothing and continued their journey to the Platte satisfied that the pursuit had been halted. Not only had they been wrong, but their pursuers had closed the gap between them during the day. Not surprising, considering that the Canary girl and the Texan could alternate between reserve horses, while the two men had but one animal apiece.

Becoming aware of Hogue's actions, Ruiz inquired, "Do you think it's wise, *amigo*?"

"Huh?" the burly man grunted, pausing with the Winchester halfway to his shoulder. "What d'you mean?"

"Is shooting them down *here* any answer?"

"How d'you mean?"

"Silvers is not one of The Outfit. If murder is done at his place, he will inform the law," Ruiz explained. "There are peace officers in Lexington to the west and Kearney to the east."

"Only we ain't going to either place," Hogue pointed out, feeling annoyed as always when the Mexican showed signs of smart thinking.

"No. We are going to Hollick City, which also has a telegraph office and sheriff," Ruiz answered. "A sheriff who knows us and would recognize our descriptions, *amigo*."

"Day Leckenby don't worry me none!" Hogue blustered, but did not complete the raising of the rifle. "He could make fuss for the boss, though."

"*Si,*" Ruiz agreed. "Needless fuss, when there is a better way."

"Such as?"

"Such as riding on——"

"You're figuring on making a run for Hollick

City?" Hogue snorted. "It's still a good day's ride and these hosses ain't getting any fresher, way we've been pushing 'em. Comes another point, I don't cotton to the notion of going back there and telling the boss that the Canary gal's trailing along with a Texas gun-slick."

"He's not *Cabrito*," Ruiz said. "I thought that he was, back in Mulrooney, but not any more."

"Whether he's the Ysabel Kid or not don't make too much difference," Hogue stated. "If he bust by Spatz's bunch, he's good with a gun."

"But he is not *Cabrito, amigo.* Which means that we can carry out my plan."

"I ain't heard no plan yet," Hogue growled, watching the riders halt at the hitching rail where their own mounts had been standing while they went into the main building for a meal. "The boss ain't going to like it one lil bit if we get back with that redheaded calico-cat still living."

From the expression on Ruiz's face, he was for once in complete agreement with his companion. They both knew that their efforts in Mulrooney had not been entirely crowned with success. Especially when they considered how much money their employer must have spent in obtaining the specialized services of The Outfit.

The partial failure was Hogue's and Ruiz's fault, for The Outfit had done their part. It had been understood from the start that, with the delicate nature of the political situation at the State

capitol, The Outfit could not arrange for Martha
Jane Canary's death in Topeka. Instead it had
been fixed so that she should be sent to meet an
honest lawyer, unconnected with the organization,
in Mulrooney and placed in a hotel where the two
men could find her.

Except for one slight snag, everything had gone
according to plan. Not being sure what the girl
looked like, and wishing to avoid mistakes, Smith
had been sent by his superior to watch the railroad
depot. For some reason, he had failed to see her
leave the train. So they had not been aware of the
nature of their intended victim. Waiting until after
midnight, Smith had escorted Hogue and Ruiz to
the Railroad House Hotel. They had discovered
which room she occupied by reading the register
on the unattended desk.

Hogue's mistrust of Mexicans had caused them
to disagree on the best way to handle the situation.
So they had decided that Ruiz should try to gain
access via the door, using a trick he had learned as
a boy, while Hogue attempted to enter through the
bedroom window. Once inside, they were to kill
the girl and carry off every document that might
prove her identity. After producing a ladder for
Hogue and pointing out the window of Room
Fourteen, Smith had left them to do their work.

The attempt had turned into a miserable fiasco.
However, Smith's superior had suggested a way by
which they might still be able to carry out the or-

ders. They could stop her reaching Counselor Talbot's office later that morning. To avoid mistakes, Smith had arranged for the hotel's desk clerk to direct the girl by a specific route to the lawyer's office. The man had remained opposite the hotel and the clerk had signaled when the correct female left.

Although the Texan's intervention had prevented them from doing more than steal the girl's documents, The Outfit's senior representative had insisted that the two men left Mulrooney without delay. He had promised that he would telegraph warning of any pursuit to Spatz's way station. Knowing the penalty for disobeying The Outfit, Hogue and Ruiz had not argued. They felt that they had carried out their orders adequately, if not entirely. If Talbot followed Lawyer Endicott's instructions, he would only tell the girl about the Rafter C when satisfied that she had the right to know about it. Somehow she had convinced the Mulrooney lawyer that she was Martha Jane Canary, and followed them accompanied by a man. Most likely he was the same fast-moving Texan who had saved her life.

It had been Hogue's suggestion that they hire Spatz's men to prevent the following pair from continuing the journey. Although harboring suspicions about the identity of the Texan, Ruiz had not argued the point. Now that the attempt had failed, the Mexican felt it was time that he take control of the situation.

"We'll stop them," Ruiz stated. "Not here and now, but on the trail."

"You mean lay for 'em and down 'em as they ride by?"

"That would be chancy, they might escape. I think it is better that we wait until tonight. Then we'll take them while they sleep."

"Great!" Hogue sniffed, returning his rifle to its boot. "How do we find 'em when they've bedded down?"

The girl and her companion had disappeared into the way station's main building, so the two men turned their horses.

"That will take some thought," Ruiz admitted as they set the animals moving. "But it should not be beyond the ability of intelligent men like us. Let us figure that they will not be less than ninety minutes, or more than two-and-a-half hours behind us when they leave Silvers'. Then, toward sundown, we will look for places where riders about that far behind would make camp. After that, we find a high place close at hand and watch for them to come."

"Like we done last night?" Hogue said coldly.

"No. We will be in position before night falls, so that we can see for sure where they camp. Riding relay, they will both be very tired. So we let them get soundly asleep and move in silently as ghosts. The man we must kill straight away, but it won't sorrow me if we take the girl alive."

"You're a mean, horny devil, Otón," Hogue grinned. "Only, what she did to your wedding-tackle in Mulrooney, I didn't reckon you'd want her that way."

Cold, savage evil played across the Mexican's face and he reached involuntarily toward the place where Calamity's knee had landed. Hard riding had done nothing to lessen the ache he felt.

"She will pay for that!" the Mexican promised.

Grinning at his companion, Hogue urged the bay gelding to a faster pace. Ruiz made the *sabino* equal it and they pushed on to the north through the rolling plains between the Plane and South Loup Rivers. Once again they kept a watch to the rear, but saw nothing of their pursuers. Neither spoke much during the journey. When the appointed time came, Ruiz suggested that they should start to look for possible places which might appeal to the other two as camp-sites.

For about a mile, no location struck them as being suitable. Then Ruiz reined in his *sabino* and pointed ahead.

"They won't get much farther and will most likely camp somewhere down there."

Following the direction indicated by his companion, Hogue nodded. At that point the stage-trail dipped into a valley. Crossing a stream in the middle, the wheel-ruts of the coaches turned upstream along the opposite bank. Although the other side of the valley had a covering of woods, its bottom was fairly open. The area would have considerable appeal for travelers who could not reach the way station on the South Loup by nightfall. It had good water and grazing for the horses, shelter and some protection against the elements.

"Could be," Hogue grudgingly conceded. "There's plenty of places where we can keep watch on the other side."

"If we go right on to where the valley curves," Ruiz remarked as they rode down the slope, "we will be able to see them no matter where they camp. Their fire will guide us back."

"If they light one," Hogue grunted, refusing to admit, even to himself, that the Mexican made right good sense. "They didn't last night."

"We didn't see it last night," Ruiz corrected patiently.

Keeping to the stage-trail so as to avoid leaving tracks that might attract unwanted curiosity, they reached the stream. After allowing the horses to drink, they pushed on along the valley. About a quarter of a mile after leaving the ford, Ruiz nodded to a hollow in the near-side slope. Fringed with bushes, its base offered a good-sized area of free ground.

"It'd be a good place to bed down," Hogue agreed. "Happen they come this far, I'd bet this's where they'll pick."

Continuing for almost another half a mile, they left the trail instead of following it around the curve. Riding up the incline through the trees, they reached the top and dismounted. After taking care of their horses, and making certain that the animals would not be seen from the bottom of the valley, the two men moved to a position from which they could watch the trail. They could not chance lighting a fire to cook food or brew coffee, a fact that increased the burly white man's hatred of their pursuers. Hogue consoled himself with the thought that they would be able to make use of the other two's property later that night.

About two hours after the two men had settled down on either side of a big old cottonwood tree's trunk, with the sun sinking in the west, they saw the girl and Texan appear on the other side. Leading their reserve horses, they rode down the stage-trail. A savage grin twisted Ruiz's lips at the sight. Clearly the pair suspected nothing, they were acting too casual and incautious for that.

With the horses watered, they crossed the stream. Riding toward the curve, they were looking about them. On drawing level with the mouth of the opening, the girl pointed to it and spoke to her companion. Apparently they shared the two men's opinion of the spot, for they turned their horses toward it. Once they had entered the hollow, the couple passed out of the watchers' range of vision. However, there was no way they could leave without being seen, so Hogue and Ruiz felt no concern.

"They've played into our hands, *amigo*," Ruiz stated.

"We may's well get some rest, then," Hogue answered.

"You go. I'll watch for a while," Ruiz suggested.

Accepting his companion's advice without argument, for once, Hogue backed off the rim. Ruiz watched for a short time longer. A movement among the trees caught his attention. Looking closer, he discovered it was caused by the girl as she moved about the slope above the hollow collecting firewood. Shortly after she had disappeared again, the Mexican saw the glow and smoke of a fire. Nodding his satisfaction, Ruiz withdrew and joined Hogue. They spread their blankets and settled down to rest.

At midnight, Ruiz stirred and sat up. Coming to his feet, he woke the other man. Hogue crawled from his blankets, cursing and scratching at his belly. Going to their horses, after folding their bedrolls, they saddled up. When all was ready for their departure, Ruiz stood for a moment, testing the wind.

"It's blowing along the valley, not across," the Mexican decided. "We can take our horses closer."

"Don't see why not," Hogue agreed. The wind would not carry their mounts' scent to the animals in the hollow. "Let's get going."

Leading their horses, the two men went on foot along the rim. They took their bearings from the faint glow of red below. When almost directly above its source, they came to a halt under the low-hanging branches of a white oak. Dropping their split-ended reins was all that they needed to do to prevent the animals straying. Range-trained, their mounts would not try to roam while the reins dangled loose to catch the feet. Glancing at Ruiz, Hogue drew the rifle from his saddle-boot. The big man still remembered the bullet whizzing by his head as he had entered the alley behind the Railroad House. So he did not intend to take unnecessary chances with the girl. Recalling how the Texan had reacted to Smith's attack, Ruiz nodded his approval and drew his own Winchester.

If their approach along the rim had been made carefully, it did not come close to the caution they showed as they descended the slope. Finding a game trail, they inched through the head-high bushes until they received their first view of their victims' camp. Still in the shelter of the bushes, they studied the scene before them.

Although dying down, the fire threw a pool of light over the center of the clearing. The couple were camped sufficiently far in the open for the men to feel pleased that they had brought their rifles and did not need to rely on handguns. A movement near the mouth of the hollow drew the two men's gaze. They saw the girl's and Texan's horses picketed close to the opening. Looking at the animals, Ruiz remembered something he had heard

about *Cabrito*. His last doubts were wiped away.
According to all the stories, the Ysabel Kid did not
need to fasten up his white stallion; but left it free
to act as a roving sentinel while he slept. The
Texan's white horse was fastened to a sapling not
far from the other mounts.

"They've sure got themselves made comfortable," Hogue whispered, diverting Ruiz's thoughts
from the horses.

Turning his eyes in the direction of the fire, the
Mexican felt inclined to agree with his companion.
Carefully he studied the blanket-covered figures
lying at the edge of the lighted area. Although the
three saddles formed an n-shaped shelter which hid
the sleepers' heads from the watchers, the outlines
of their bodies showed plain enough beneath the
blankets. From all appearances, they were
bundling belly to belly and in each other's arms.
The young man's back was toward Hogue and
Ruiz, his shoulder exposed above the coverings
and arm draped across the girl. Their boots stood
by the foot of the temporary bed and their hats
hung on the horns of the riding saddles. Hanging
across the seats of the saddles, the two gun-belts
were so positioned that the watchers could see the
revolvers in their holsters.

"If we shoot him, the bullets will go through
and kill the girl," Ruiz warned Hogue in a soft
voice.

"You'll have to chance it," the white man

replied, no louder. Even as he spoke, they saw the sleeping Texan's arm move a little. "Take them!"

Swinging up their rifles, they lined the sights. Two shots rang out at almost the same instant, lighting the night with their muzzle-blasts and slamming echoes along the valley. Through the whirling powder-smoke, Hogue and Ruiz watched the blankets agitate as the bullets ripped through into the back of the male sleeper. Although his body jerked under the impact, neither he nor the girl attempted to rise or even moved.

"Got 'em both, like I figured!" Hogue announced, working his rifle's loading lever and striding from the bushes.

Following the white man, Ruiz fed another live round into his Winchester. As soon as they had made sure that the couple were dead, the Mexican planned to take care of the insulting *gringo* and be the only one of them to return to claim the rewards for their work.

Chapter 9

TAKE HIM ALIVE

~~~

"YOU RUINED MY SHIRT."

Soft spoken, gentle almost, though they were, the words which came from the right of the advancing pair sounded charged with menace and bore a deadly warning. With sickening impact, Hogue and Ruiz knew that something had gone terribly wrong.

Turning his head in the direction of the speaker, Ruiz let out a savage snarl that combined anger with superstitious fear. Two figures had stepped from the bushes about thirty yards from where the would-be killers had come to a sudden halt. Dressed as she had been on the street in Mulrooney, except for her kepi and gunbelt being missing and moccasins instead of boots on her feet, the girl gripped a Winchester carbine ready for use.

Bare-headed, rifle in hands, the Texan wore all black clothing and had the face of a scalp-hunting *Pehnane* Dog Soldier. The bowie knife that usually rode on his gunbelt swung sheathed from his waistband.

"Cabrito!" Ruiz croaked.

The words jolted through the shock that had numbed Hogue into immobility. With a curse, he started to swing in the couple's direction and whip the rifle to his shoulder. Throwing off his fears and thoughts on how the figure in the bed had moved its arm, Ruiz copied his companion's move. Already the Kid's Winchester was rising in a lightning-fast, smoothly flowing motion. His right eye squinted along the barrel as the butt settled into place. While Calamity was still raising the lighter carbine, the Kid squeezed his old yellow-boy's trigger.

Once again gunfire illuminated and shattered the silence of the darkness. Twice in a second the Kid's Winchester cracked, its lever blurring down then up between the shots so fast that the eye could barely follow the movements. Firing at such speed did not allow for a change in the point of aim. So, even as he turned loose his second bullet, the Kid was relying on Calamity to stop Ruiz shooting him. Both the girl's and the Mexican's weapons were lining and the Kid's life hung in a very delicate balance.

Wanting a living prisoner whom they could question, the Kid had shot to wound rather than kill. Hogue was the faster of the pair to recover, so he received first attention. Both of the Kid's bullets ripped into the right side of the burly man's chest, spinning him around in a full circle. The rifle flew from Hogue's hands and he stumbled in front of Ruiz just as the Mexican laid sights on the Kid. Unable to stop himself, Ruiz completed his pressure on the trigger. He saw flame lance from his rifle's muzzle and a hole appear in the center of Hogue's back.

The same accident that saved the Kid had a beneficial effect on Ruiz. A split second after the Mexican fired, Calamity's carbine spoke. Meant for Ruiz, the bullet spiked into the center of the reeling white man's chest. Yet the Mexican knew that he was far from out of the woods. Staggering on, Hogue collapsed face down and left his companion exposed to Calamity's and the Kid's weapons. Already the dark Texan had sent another bullet into his rifle's chamber and was changing the direction in which its muzzle pointed.

Discarding his rifle as a useless encumbrance to his escape, Ruiz hurled himself toward the bushes. He moved just in time to avoid catching the Kid's next bullet. Calamity's carbine swung and spat. Jerking from his head, Ruiz's *sombrero* spun away. When he did not fall or break stride, she knew that she had hit the hat but missed its wearer. Throwing her lever through its reloading cycle, she wondered why the Kid did not use his rifle to bring down the fleeing man.

"Watch that 'n', gal!" the Kid barked, lowering the Winchester and laying it on the ground. "I'm going after the other. I want to take him alive."

Before Calamity could debate the point, even if she had wished to do so, the Kid went racing into the bushes where Ruiz had already disappeared. Watching him go, Calamity gave a low hiss of anxiety. She hoped the Kid had not forgotten that he had only his bowie knife and Ruiz packed a revolver on his belt. Putting the thought from her mind, she turned her attention to the clearing. Alert for any hostile move on his part, she walked toward Hogue. There was no need for precautions. The Kid's two bullets might not have killed him, but either of the others would have been fatal. If the Kid wanted somebody to answer questions, it would have to be the Mexican.

Crashing through the bushes, Ruiz went up the slope as fast as his legs would carry him. At any moment he expected to feel lead driving into his body, but it did not come. So he gave a thought to what would be his best line of action. Stopping to avenge Hogue never entered his head; his main aim as he ran was to save his own skin. If he could reach the horses and mount up, he stood a better than fair chance of making it. Fast though *Cabrito*'s white stallion was reputed to be, there would be a delay while he collected and freed it. During the time he spent doing it, Ruiz would be building up a lead. Using Hogue's bay and his *sabino* to ride relay, he could press on fast, reach Hollick City and get help to deal with the Kid and the girl.

Having decided on what to do, he approached the horses. They still stood patiently under the white oak. Going between them, he grabbed hold of the bay's reins in his right hand. Taking up the *sabino*'s reins in his left, he inserted his left foot into the stirrup, gripped the dinner-plate horn of his Mexican saddle in both hands and started to mount. Even as he swung himself astride, he heard the soft pad of rapidly approaching feet and remembered that, like the girl, the Kid had been wearing moccasins.

For all his advantage in footwear, the Kid had not been able to catch up with the fleeing Mexican on the slope. Seeing the man mounting, the Kid launched himself into the air. Reaching upward, his hands hooked over one of the tree's lowest branches. With a surging swing, the Kid propelled himself at Ruiz. Two feet smashed into the Mexican's shoulder. Barely mounted, Ruiz felt himself struck by the Kid's flying body and tilted sideways. Startled by its rider's unexpected behavior, the *sabino* lunged forward. Taken with the Kid's attack, the motion unseated Ruiz. Unsettled by the disturbance, the bay followed the *sabino*. Missing its departing rump, the two men plunged to the ground.

Going down in a rolling dive, the Kid parted company with Ruiz. Surprised as he had been, the Mexican recovered fast. Regardless at first of their trailing reins, the horses plunged off into the trees. Ignoring them for the moment, the Kid concentrated on the Mexican. They made their feet at almost the same instant, facing each other in the darkness.

Two right hands flashed to the hilt of knives and steel glinted faintly under the pale light of the stars. Even as Ruiz saw the Kid start moving toward him, he felt elation rise inside him. White men in general, and Texans in particular, tended to regard Mexicans as knife- rather than gun-fighters. It was a belief that Ruiz had used to his advantage on more than one occasion. His white opponents had expected him to make his play with cold steel rather than hot lead. That expectation had cost four men their lives.

What Ruiz failed to take into consideration was that the Kid was only part-white. Both the French-Creoles and the Comanches had long been knife-fighters. In addition to that, the Kid had been around Mexicans long and often enough to know that some of them were good with handguns.

Taking in the other's stance, the Kid's mind screamed a warning. Ruiz's foot placement was wrong. Correct for using a gun, but not offering the freedom of balance and movement needed when fighting with a knife.

Even as the thought came, Ruiz dropped the knife, and his right hand flew down to the Colt's butt. Up tilted the long barrel, still in its holster and the hammer clicked back under Ruiz's thumb. The trigger had been removed, so he had only to release the hammer to fire.

No white man could have saved himself, but at that moment the Kid was pure, unadulterated *Pehnane* Dog Soldier. Only an arm's length separated them when the Colt's cocking click reached his ears. Already he had remembered what kind of holster Ruiz used, recognizing its advantages and limitations. While such a rig allowed its user to get off a shot very fast, it severely restricted the mobility of the revolver.

With the sound of the click registering in his ears, the Kid twisted his body sideways and to Ruiz's left. He heard the crash of the shot and felt the heat of the muzzle-flare against his back, but the bullet scraped by his shirt without touching him. In a flash, the Kid retaliated. Up that close, he did not dare hesitate. Nor, if it came to the point, could he halt the instantaneous response the narrow escape from death triggered off.

Lashing back and up with his right hand, the Kid swung his bowie knife in a savage chop. He turned his torso, adding force to the blow. The razor-edged, eleven-and-a-half-inch-long, two-

and-a-half-inch-wide blade passed under Ruiz's chin and bit deep into his throat. Blood spurted from the terrible, mortal wound and the man stumbled backward. Releasing the butt of his Colt, the right hand rose to join the left in a futile attempt to stop the life-blood gushing from the bone-deep tear in his throat.

The blow had been struck by a Comanche, a name-warrior of the dreaded *Pehnane* Dog Soldier war lodge. So deeply had the training of his childhood been ingrained into his being that the Kid could not have halted his reaction to the Mexican's shot. Nor could he hold down the coup-cry which followed the delivery of the blow.

"A:he!" the Kid growled in guttural Comanche, meaning, "I claim it!"

Standing balanced lightly on the balls of his feet, body crouched in a knife-fighter's stance, the Kid allowed the savage passions of a *Nemenuh* braveheart to ebb away. Then he looked around him. Ruiz lay huddled against the trunk of a tree, spasmodic movements of his limbs growing weaker. Not far away, the *sabino* had come to a halt with its reins tangled in a bush. It stood snorting and trying to free itself while the bay ran on, but more slowly.

"Damn it!" the Kid grunted, walking over to Ruiz's body. "He sure won't be telling us anything."

Yet there had been no other way to handle the

situation. Men like Ruiz had no compunction about killing and were deadly dangerous as long as they lived. Up so close, if he had not been stopped, he could have turned the holster far enough to make a hit with his next bullet. So the Kid had stopped him, swiftly, effectively—but permanently.

Kneeling by the corpse, the Kid searched it. He did not find Calamity's letter. So, after cleaning the blade of his knife on Ruiz's jacket, he rose and walked across to the *sabino*. Soothing it, he freed the reins and swung into the saddle. Although he knew that Calamity would be raising a muck-sweat of anxiety, having heard the shot and being aware that he did not carry a firearm, he rode after the bay. Catching Hogue's horse, he gathered in its reins and led it back in the direction of the hollow.

Everything looked quiet and peaceful as the Kid came into sight of their camp. Hogue's body sprawled where it had fallen, the horses still stood quietly on the picket lines and the blanket-covered mounds were by the fire. However, there was no sign of Calamity or the Kid's rifle.

Hearing a sound from the bushes to his left, the Kid swung in that direction. Calamity walked from the undergrowth, carrying her carbine in one hand and his rifle in the other. Relief showed on her face as she came toward the Kid and he dropped from the *sabino*'s saddle.

"When I heard the hosses coming, after that shot, I didn't know which way it'd gone," she explained. "So I got out of sight until I knowed who'd won. Can't say I'm sorry to see it's you."

"I didn't get him alive 'n' talking," the Kid admitted. "Hold on to these hosses while I search his *amigo*. Otón wasn't carrying your letter."

Taking the horses' reins. Calamity watched the Kid search Hogue's body with the precision of a trained peace officer. Failing to produce the documents, he asked her to help him with the animals. After they had unsaddled the bay and *sabino,* they hobbled all but the white stallion. Hobbling was to be preferred to using a picket line. With their front legs secured by two cuffs connected by a short swivel chain, the horses could move around slowly, graze, but not wander too far. The stallion was set free and moved off, snorting a little.

"Damned if ole Nigger ain't riled because he's been tied up for once," Calamity grinned.

"We had to do it," the Kid answered. "Else he'd've heard them coming and either got shot charging 'em, or scared 'em off."

Despite Hogue's and Ruiz's thoughts, their pursuers had not been unaware of the danger. In fact Calamity and the Kid had become aware how close behind they were on their arrival at Silvers' way station.

The previous night, Calamity and the Kid had made a carefully concealed camp. Leaving it early, they had continued their swift progress along the stage-trail. On reaching the way station, they had found proof of the men's proximity. Newly left horse-droppings at the hitching rail gave a warning that was augmented by the presence of two sets of plates and cups on a table. Small things in themselves, but sufficient to tell them that the men they sought had passed that way recently. Maybe so recently that they had seen Calamity and the Kid ride up. If so, they would know that Spatz's attempt had failed and decide to take action themselves.

When the Kid had tried to raise the matter of the previous visitors, the Silvers' family had proved uncommunicative. While honest enough, the agent also possessed a streak of sensible caution. He had read the signs and known that the two hard-cases were expecting, or at least ready for somebody to arrive. As long as the trouble did not erupt on his property, Silvers did not intend to become involved.

Respecting Silvers' reticence, Calamity and the Kid had restricted themselves to the first evasively answered questions. They had eaten a meal, rested and grain-fed their horses. Then, after purchasing sufficient food to last them until they reached Hollick City, they had ridden on. Keeping up a fast pace, they had been even more alert for the possibility of an ambush. Not that the Kid expected the attempt to be made in daylight. Even without knowing that he was followed by *Cabrito,* the Mexican would most likely insist on playing things safe. Either the men would keep going, intending to collect reinforcements at Hollick City, or make their move after dark.

From his first view of the valley, the Kid had guessed that the Mexican would go for the latter alternative. With his extensive knowledge of men like Ruiz, the Kid had accurately followed the other's line of thought. Discussing the matter while riding down the southern slope, the girl and the Kid had decided that their chances of retrieving her letter would be better that night than after it had been delivered to whoever hired the men. So they elected to lay a trap in the hope of luring Hogue and Ruiz into their clutches.

Riding along the valley, they selected the camp-site in the hollow as the one best suited to their needs. Already the Kid had located the watching men and guessed at their intentions.

Although Ruiz had seen Calamity at her wood-gathering, he had failed to notice that the Kid also left the clearing. Taking advantage of every scrap of cover, the Texan had examined the surrounding area to make sure that their enemies could not see what went on beyond the bushes. Satisfied on that point, he had rejoined the girl. They had lit a fire and made their preparations. Not wanting the horses wandering about the clearing, they had set up a picket line in a place from which the attackers were unlikely to come.

Working fast, Calamity and the Kid had made two dummies out of their spare clothes stuffed with grass and bush-branches. The Kid had changed shirts, using the one the men had seen him wearing to clothe the "man." Arranging the saddles to hide the fact that the dummies had no heads, they had covered the "bodies" with a blanket and placed the "man's" arm across the "woman's" shoulders. The hats, gunbelts with revolvers in plain view, and boots had been placed to give the impression that the girl and the Texan slept by the fire.

There had been one more touch added to convey an air of life to the dummies. Borrowing a reel of stout black cotton thread that Calamity had in her *parfleche,* the Kid had attached its end to the "male" dummy's exposed shirt-sleeve. Unwinding the cotton as he backed across to the bushes, he had tested its part in the deception. On being tugged gently, the thread of cotton had caused the sleeve to move as if the "man" was stirring in his sleep.

Maybe the dummies would not have worked in the light of day, but they had proved realistic enough when seen by the faint glow of the fire. Taking cover, Calamity and the Kid had waited for the men to come.

"Seeing's how I'm all set to be a rich rancher," Calamity remarked as she took the dummies to pieces, looking to where the Kid was unrolling and searching Otón's belongings, "I'll stand treat on a new shirt for you."

"*Gracias,*" grinned the Kid. "That letter ain't here. Unless it's in the other feller's gear, you won't get to be a rich rancher. You won't be able to prove to that law-wrangler in Hollick City that you're Martha Jane Canary."

"It'll be easy enough," Calamity stated.

"How come?" inquired the Kid, completing the repacking of the Mexican's bedroll and opening Hogue's.

"Why, I'll just look at him right truthful and tell him who I am."

"What if it don't work?"

"Then I'll whomp the son-of-a-bitch over the head with my whip-handle for not trusting a sweet, loving-natured gal like me," Calamity replied. Seeing a familiar object fall from Hogue's up-ended warbag, she pounced on it. "Yahoo! Here's my letter, Lon!" She opened the envelope and looked inside. "They're there. Now I can prove I'm me."

"Was I you, knowing you the way I do," the Kid replied, "That'd plumb give me the miseries."

"You watch your mouth," Calamity warned. "Us rich ranchers all stick together. More of your uncivilness, and I'll ask Ole Devil to put you riding the blister end of a shovel when you get back to home."

"Being rich hasn't changed you, gal," the Kid announced. "You're still the same ornery, perverse cuss you allus was."

"And I'm right proud of it," Calamity grinned. Then she became more serious. "Anything to say who sent them after me, Lon?"

"Nothing's I can find," the Kid replied, after completing a search.

"What're we going to do, then?"

"Get us some sleep."

"I mean tomorrow!" Calamity snorted.

"Keep going, gal," the Kid told her. "We'll take their hosses 'n' gear along with us. I'll be kind of interested to see who takes notice of us bringing them into Hollick City."

Chapter 10

I'D SAY THEY WAS EXPECTING TROUBLE

LEAVING THE TWO BODIES SO THAT ANY INTERESTED peace officer could come out and check their story of the incident, Calamity and the Kid continued along the trail to Hollick City. They had spent the night in the clearing, moving on soon after dawn. Calling in at the South Loup River way station, they had attracted no interest from having the *sabino* and bay along. So they had pushed on, holding to the same pace that had covered at least sixty miles a day since leaving Mulrooney. In the middle of the afternoon, they saw the sun glinting on the roofs of their destination. Built on the banks of the Middle Loup River, under the slopes of a wood-covered hill range, the town looked small

and unimpressive in comparison with Mulrooney.
It was still a good three miles away and, not far
ahead of them, Calamity and the Kid saw a narrow
track branching from the trail. Hardly more than
the marks caused by a solitary wagon and a few
horses going back and forward, the track turned
off beyond a big old cottonwood tree and continued across the range in the direction of the hills.

Going by the tree, Calamity and the Kid saw a
piece of wood nailed to it. Halting their horses,
they looked at the letters burned into the wooden
indicator that pointed along the track.

"/C\ONE MILE"

"That's the Rafter C brand, gal," the Kid announced. "I'd say your ranch house's a mile along
that track."

They looked in the required direction. The land
rolled away in undulating green folds until it
joined the hills perhaps five miles from the stage-
trail. There was no sign of the house or other ranch
buildings. However, smoke rose from behind a
ridge about a mile away. Not the black cloud of an
unchecked fire, but a single plume such as might
rise from a chimney.

"There's somebody at home," Calamity declared. "Maybe it's pappy——"

"And maybe it's not," warned the Kid. "If your
pappy was still there, likely the lawyer in Hollick
City wouldn't've needed to start hunting for you to
make his offer."

"Then whoever's there shouldn't be!" Calamity snorted and made as if to set her horses moving.

"Hold hard there, you damned hothead!" barked the Kid, reaching out a hand to catch hold of her arm. "We don't know who's there, what they're doing there, or how many of them's doing it. Could be whoever it is's got what they reckon's a real good reason for being there."

"And could be they ain't!"

"I'm not gainsaying it, gal. So we'll just drift over there casual-like and see what's doing. They don't know who-all we are. So leave us not go in there with heads down and horns a-hooking when riding up peaceable'll let us learn more."

Accepting the wisdom of the Kid's suggestion, Calamity accompanied him along the track. They saw only a few bunches of cattle, but several fair-sized bands of horses were grazing on what would probably be the ranch's territory.

"It's good range, Calam," the Kid commented. "Been well-tended. If all them critters carry the Rafter C, it's got a fair head of stock. Six thousand'd be a low price if the rest's this good."

"I'd reckon so," the girl replied. "What I can't get over is pappy owning a spread this good. He wasn't one to take to hard-sweating work, way Maw allus told us kids."

Coming into sight of the ranch's buildings did nothing to change their opinion of Calamity's property. The main house was small, but sturdily

built and recently repainted. Behind it stretched a
carefully cultivated truck-garden that would more
than supply the ranch's needs for vegetables. All
the other buildings and structures showed the same
care in upkeep. There was a combined barn,
hayloft and stable of fair size, a small blacksmith's
forge, a bunkhouse. Along by the creek that curled
about the dwellings, pigs grunted in half a dozen
pens. Four corrals ranged to the north of the
house. Studying them, the Kid had his theory, that
the ranch specialized in horses rather than cattle,
confirmed. Two of the pole-built enclosures had
chutes attached in which unbroken horses could be
saddled and mounted, and a snubbing-post rose in
the center of the third.

Suddenly a large bluetick hound burst from the
open door of the house. Making the air ring with
its baying, it sprang across the porch and headed
toward the two riders.

"Sam!" shouted a male voice and the hound
came to a stop, but remained menacingly watchful.

Followed by a woman, a tall, wide-shouldered
young man came from the house. Ruggedly good-
looking, he had no hat on his rumpled brown hair,
but wore range clothes. The Army Colt at his right
thigh rode in a well-designed, tied-down holster
and he gave the impression of being able to utilize
both to their full potential.

The woman was medium height, slim, pretty
and had hair as red as Calamity's. Wiping flour

from her hands on to the apron covering her ging-
ham frock, she looked at the newcomers. Then she
spoke quietly to the man.

"Come ahead," he called. "Sam won't hurt you."

Having halted at the sight of the dog, Calamity
and the Kid started their horses moving. Darting
quick glances around, the Kid noticed a be-
whiskered, leathery old-timer leaning against the
bunkhouse door and nursing a Spencer carbine on
the crook of his left arm. A younger cowhand
stood just inside the barn's open double doors, his
right hand thumb-hooked in his gunbelt close to
the butt of an Army Colt. Up above him, at the entrance to the hayloft, a second young cowhand
watched the approaching couple with the same
alert air that all the other men showed.

Of course one could expect folks to show curiosity when visitors came calling, but there was
more than ordinary, casual interest in the way the
people on the ranch watched Calamity and the
Kid. Having seen the signs, Calamity flashed a
glance at her companion.

"I'd say they was expecting trouble," she commented *sotto-voce*.

"Then don't you go starting it," warned the Kid
in no louder tones.

"As if *I* would!" Calamity whispered.

Going past the hound, they halted their horses in
front of the couple. The Kid took off his hat and
addressed the man and woman.

"Howdy, folks. We found this *sabino* 'n' bay straying back down the trail a ways and was wondering if they'd come from here."

Looking at the two horses, the man paid most attention to the *sabino* and its distinctive Mexican-style saddle. There was a strong hint of suspicion as he swung his eyes from the horse. He seemed to be studying the land behind Calamity and the Kid before he answered, and when he spoke, his voice was cold, unfriendly.

"They don't belong here."

That appeared to end the matter as far as he was concerned. Which struck the Kid as peculiar, if not downright suspicious. A saddled, riderless horse had always been a cause of grave concern in the West. Left afoot, a man could be in serious danger. So folks mostly displayed interest on being told that a horse had been found straying. The man did not appear to care, although two such animals were involved.

"Coffee's on the boil," the woman put in, running her eyes over Calamity's travel-stained, hard-ridden appearance. "You look like you could do with a cup and a hot meal."

"Thanks," Calamity replied. "I could use both, happen you'd let me help you make 'em."

"Light and rest your saddles," the man offered, just a touch reluctantly. "Water your hosses at the trough, then come on in."

"He knowed that *sabino,*" Calamity told the Kid as they went to follow the man's instructions. "And he sure don't act sociable."

"Maybe he's got his reasons," the Kid replied. "So don't you go letting on who you are and maybe we'll find out what's up."

With their horses' welfare attended to, Calamity and the Kid rejoined the couple before the house. The bluetick sat between the man and the woman, looking as unfriendly as a buffalo-wolf. Glancing around, the Kid saw that the cowhands had resumed their interrupted work.

"That's a real fine horse, mister," the man said, nodding to the Kid's stallion. "He wouldn't be for sale, would he?"

"Had him so long he's plumb ruined for decent company," the Kid answered.

"You look as if you've covered some miles," the woman said, directing her words to the girl.

"Come up from Mulrooney," Calamity replied. "I'm meeting my boss' freight outfit when it comes through. I'm Calamity Jane and this's the Ysabel Kid."

The man and woman looked from one to the other of their visitors. If anything, Calamity was the better known to them, although something of the Kid's fame appeared to have spread to Nebraska. Some of the suspicion left the man's face, but it still held a wary look.

"I'm Cash Trinian," he said, with a hint of challenge in his voice and his right hand dangling by the Colt's butt. "This's my wife, Corey-Mae."

"I won't make out I've not heard of you," drawled the Kid, holding forward his right hand. "But the War's long over and best forgot."

For a moment Trinian hesitated. Then he nodded and took the offered hand in his. "Like you say, Kid, it's long over and best forgot. Only there's some on both sides haven't forgotten."

"Cash rode with Lane's Red-Legs in the War, Calamity," Corey-Mae explained.

Not that she needed to do so. Calamity remembered stories of Cash Trinian during the War between the States. In those days he had won a reputation as a fast-drawing, hard-riding member of Lane's band of Union guerillas, an outfit every bit as vicious, bloodthirsty and murderous as Dixie's Quantrill's raiders. Yet there had been decent youngsters riding with each of the outfits, believing that they were serving their side's cause. Cash Trinian had been one of them. After the War, the fast-gun name had stuck. Such a man might be wary when a strange Texan, of a breed noted for being gun-fighters, came calling unexpectedly.

"The Kid was with Mosby," Calamity replied disinterestedly. "Anyways, men're allus doing some fool thing like going to fighting where us women'd set down and talk it out peaceable."

"Yeah, Cash," grinned the Kid. "She *is* Calamity Jane. Even if she just said that mouthful."

"Come in and rest your feet." Corey-Mae smiled. "I agree with Calamity."

"Now she won't be fit to talk to for a week," groaned the Kid.

Stepping aside, the Trinians let Calamity and the Kid enter the house's parlor. The room had good-quality furnishings and was clean, but not to the point of discomfort. Clearly Corey-Mae took as much pride in her home as her husband appeared to in the upkeep of the ranch. Telling her husband to make their guests comfortable, Corey-Mae bustled off into the kitchen.

Trinian removed his gunbelt and hung it on the magnificent spread of wapiti horns fixed to the wall by the door. Following their host's example with belts and hats, Calamity and the Kid exchanged glances.

"I'll go lend Corey-Mae a hand," Calamity announced and left before Trinian could agree or object.

Waving the Kid to a chair at the table, Trinian sat across from him. The Kid offered his makings and they rolled cigarettes.

"You found them two hosses straying back there?" Trinian asked, after they had lit up their smokes.

"Yep," drawled the Kid. "Shouted some, fired off a couple of shots, trying to get an answer from whoever'd lost 'em. Even tried to back-track 'em but couldn't. So we reckoned we'd best take 'em into Hollick City and hand 'em over to the sheriff. Only we saw your place and wondered if they belonged to your hands. Reckoned you'd want to know if they did."

"They don't."

"You know who does own 'em? There can't be many folks riding Mexican saddles up this way."

"I've not seen one for some time now. Mexican called Ruiz used to ride a *sabino,* with a saddle like that, but he's not around anymore that I've seen."

"We'd best take 'em into town then," drawled the Kid. "Only there's some tin stars who'd just keep, or sell the hosses, without trying to find who owned 'em."

"Day Leckenby's not that kind!" Trinian stated flatly. "If you found them in his bailiwick, he'll do everything he can to learn where the riders are at. He's a straight lawman. I was his deputy until I come out here and I know him."

"Like you say, you'd know him," the Kid replied. "Anyways, all Calam 'n' me want to do is hand 'em over and find some place to bed down until Dobe Killem's freight outfit gets here."

"Are you going in for freighting now?"

"Nope. Only Calam's done stood by us floating outfit boys in a couple of mean fusses and I reckoned I'd see her settled safe with her folks afore I headed back to Texas. Somebody tried to kill her in Mulrooney."

"They did?" Trinian asked, looking interested.

"Twice. Once in her hotel room and again on the streets, that's how I come into it."

"Did you get the feller who tried it?"

"Sure did."

"Why'd he want to kill her?" Trinian asked.

"Had to kill him to stop him doing it," the Kid replied, watching the other's face for some emotion. "So we couldn't ask. Kail Beauregard was looking into it when we left."

If Trinian knew anything about the attempts, he hid it very well. Not wanting to arouse the other's suspicions by taking the matter further, the Kid changed the subject to the ranching prospects of Nebraska.

In the kitchen, Calamity peeled off her jacket, washed her hands and face, then went to help Corey-Mae make the meal.

"Nice place you've got here," the girl remarked. "I bet you're real proud to own it."

"We don't own it," Corey-Mae corrected while setting a skillet on the stove.

"You don't?"

"No," the woman answered, sounding a touch bitter. "We only rent it from the feller who owns it."

"Doesn't he run it?"

"That shows you don't know Howie Canary. He was a nice enough feller, but a foot-loose drifter.

Afore he left, he put the title deed to the ranch in the name of his daughter back East. That riled Cash, I can tell you."

"How come?"

"Cash wanted to buy the place. We was getting set to be married and he knew I wanted him in a safer job than a deputy sheriff."

"You wound up here, anyways," Calamity pointed out.

"Sure," Corey-Mae agreed. "We wound up here. Howie wanted hard cash for the place to send to his daughter back East. We didn't have it right then, so he told us to come out here, work the place and pay its taxes and, when we could afford it, buy it from the gal."

"Looks like you got a bargain."

"You should have seen it when we first moved out here. The whole place was tumbling apart. Cash and the boys've worked real hard to make it look this good. And it doesn't just *look* good, it's a paying proposition. What riles me is that we've done all this work and some Eastern gal who's never seen the place can take it and sell it out from under us if she feels that way inclined."

"Why don't you try buying it off her?" Calamity asked.

"We're trying to," Corey-Mae answered. "Lawyer Endicott in Hollick's sent word East trying to find this Canary gal. If he does, we're willing to pay her six thousand dollars for the place.

Hell, I know it's worth maybe three, four thousand more, but it's our work that's made it that way. And we're having to pay Pinkertons to find her. It's not a bad price, Calam, when all the ranch cost Howie was the time he spent in a poker game. He won it off the feller's used to own it."

"Getting it this good cost you a heap more than that," Calamity said softly and was about to disclose her identity when the woman's face hardened.

"It cost us too much to let anybody push us off!" Corey-Mae said harshly.

"Is somebody trying to?" Calamity inquired. "I saw the way your crew watched us as we rode in."

"Florence Eastfield, up at the sawmill, wants our land," Corey-Mae answered. "Don't ask me why. There's no timber on this side of the Loup. Not enough to make cutting it worthwhile, anyways."

"Has she been making fuss for you?"

"Not fuss, exactly. Day Leckenby, the sheriff, keeps her boys and our'n apart in town, or they might've locked horns a couple of times. Eastfield offered to buy us out. And when we told her we couldn't sell, even if we wanted to, she hinted that she could top any offer we made to the Canary gal. Damn it all, Calamity, I don't know why I'm burdening you with our troubles."

"Sometimes just talking about them helps," Calamity replied. "Food's near on done. Can I start to setting the table?"

"Go to it." Corey-Mae smiled.

Throughout the meal, the conversation was on general matters. At its end, Calamity offered to help wash the dishes.

"Maybe you'd best get those hosses took into Hollick for the sheriff," Trinian suggested.

"It'd be best," the Kid agreed. "Thanks right kindly for the meal, ma'am."

Leaving the house, Calamity and the Kid readied their horses, mounted and started to ride back along the track. Turning in her saddle, the girl waved. Corey-Mae answered, then went inside after her husband. Facing the front, Calamity told the Kid what she had learned.

"You didn't let on that you're that Canary gal from 'back East,' which's all to the good," the Kid replied, then explained that he had not learned much from Trinian. "Maybe he's just uneasy around Texans."

"I knowed there was something I liked about him, that being the case," Calamity grinned, then lost the smile. "Those folks're facing a raw deal, Lon."

"Maybe they felt like changing it," the Kid hinted.

"Not Corey-Mae!"

"Maybe not her. But Lane didn't have many angels riding with him and Cash Trinian didn't strike me as a man who'd easy give up anything he wanted."

"You just don't like Yankees," Calamity accused.

"I get on real good with *some* Yankees," the Kid corrected. "Trinian's not much of a talker. Unlikely as it is, us being so all-fired noble and easy to get on with, he mightn't like Texans. Or he may be up to something sneaky, like that play in Mulrooney. That being so, he'd be real watching with his words to somebody who'd come up from there in a hurry and'd worn a deputy's badge in town."

"You mean he hired them two jaspers?"

"Could be. He let on that he knowed a Mexican who owned a *sabino,* but no more than that. Even with what he'd have to pay The Outfit, it'd likely come out cheaper and more certain killing you rather than offering to buy you out."

"There's another player in the game, with an eye on the Rafter C," Calamity commented. "Gal who owns a sawmill across the Loup."

"Trinian never let on about her," the Kid said quietly. "Why'd somebody's owns a sawmill want ranching country?"

"Maybe we'll get a chance to ask her when we hit Hollick City," Calamity replied. "Cash recognized the *sabino*. I'll be right interested to see if that Eastfield gal shows she does."

Chapter 11

I'M GOING TO STOP YOU DEAD

A COUPLE OF TYPICAL SMALL-TOWN LOAFERS SEATED
outside the Clipper Saloon took their eyes from the
four horses at its hitching rail and looked at the
two riders coming along Hollick City's main, almost only, street. To make sure that Hogue's and
Ruiz's mounts did not go unnoticed, Calamity and
the Kid led them on the outside of their relays.
Staring at the *sabino* for a moment, one of the
loafers rose and passed hurriedly through the
batwing doors.

Giving no hint of their awareness that the *sabino*
had attracted attention, Calamity and the Kid rode
by the saloon. They turned toward the hitching rail
of the stone building with barred windows and a

sign announcing "SHERIFF'S OFFICE, Hollick City."

"There's somebody who knowed the *sabino*," drawled the Kid. "Gone to spread the word it's back, most likely."

"Them four hosses outside the saloon didn't have ropes on their saddles," Calamity replied. "Which means they don't belong to cow—— They're coming, Lon. Four of 'em."

Dismounting, the Kid slid his Winchester from its boot before tossing the horses' reins over the hitching rail. While Calamity swung down and secured her relay, he turned his eyes quickly toward the approaching men. All in all, they looked like bad medicine to run up against.

Three of them wore range clothes, but they were not cowhands. All were tall. The one slightly in the lead was best-dressed of them, swarthily handsome, with black hair. To his right, was a slightly bigger, thicker-set hard-case with ginger sidewhiskers. At the left rear, the third man was smaller than the others—which did not make him a midget—brown-haired and unshaven. One thing all had in common. They each wore their guns—a pearl-handled Smith & Wesson 1869 Army revolver in the leader's case—in tied-down holsters.

Which left the fourth of the party. Studying him as he slouched along in the rear, the Kid was willing to admit that he had a size and heft almost equal to Mark Counter. There the resemblance ended, for the man had neither Mark's handsome features nor superb build. A shaved head, creased by a long scar, did nothing to enhance a brutal, bristle-stubbled face. He hardly seemed to have any neck, but spread out to bulky shoulders that strained at his tartan shirt. There was little slimming down at his middle. He wore Levi's pants tucked into heavy, flat-heeled boots with sharp-spiked caulks in the soles. First thing to strike the Kid, though, was that he did not wear a gun. Instead, he toted a long-handled, double-headed axe that looked as sharp as many a knife.

"Hey you!" called the handsome man as Calamity swung on to the sidewalk.

"Us?" asked the Kid mildly, joining the girl.

At the sight of the rifle, held at the wrist of the butt with three fingers in the lever and the forefinger through the trigger, the man came to a halt. That was a position of readiness, allowing the weapon to be brought into action fast.

"Yeah," the man agreed. "Where'd you get the *sabino*?"

"Found it straying, along with the bay there, back along the trail," the Kid replied, facing the quartet.

"How'd they come to be straying, cow-nurse?" demanded the ginger-haired man.

"Best ask 'em," answered the Kid. "They've not told us a thing."

"Don't get smart with us, beef-head!" warned

the handsome man and indicated the fourth member of his party with his left thumb. "Olaf don't like folks who do."

"Olaf don't like it one lil bit!" rumbled the giant, hefting his axe and pushing by his companions to advance along the sidewalk.

Watching the almost babyish innocent expression on the Kid's face, Calamity inched her right hand in the direction of the whip. When he looked that way, the Kid was at instant readiness for trouble. Unless those four yahoos backed off, there was likely to be an explosion and she wanted to be set to take her part.

Studying the giant, the Kid figured that he would take a whole heap of stopping happen he meant mischief. However, the Indian-dark Texan reckoned that he held the means of doing the stopping— except that the other three *hombres* were likely to cut in the moment the big cuss made his play. Ignoring the rifle, the giant continued to advance.

There was something awesome about the bald man's behavior, hinting at a complete disregard for danger, almost animal strength and power, and a lack of fear. Behind him, the three gunslingers tensed. Maybe the giant did not recognize the Kid's potential, but they did. Yet they made no attempt to warn their companion.

"Just one more step!" thought the Kid, measuring the distance between them with his eye. "One more 'n' I'm going to stop you dead."

Every instinct warned the Kid that he would have to do just that. Nothing else would halt that brute-man before him. And then all hell would pop. Most likely Calamity would take one of the gun-hands out of the game. Possibly the Kid could account for another; but the third stood a better than even chance of making Ole Devil's floating outfit short of a member.

Even as the giant raised his foot for the step which would have caused a bullet to spike between his eyes, the office's door opened and a man stepped out. Of medium height, he had a breadth to his shoulders and powerful frame that made him look taller. He wore range clothes of good quality, clean, neat but not new. Tanned by long exposure to the elements, his heavily mustached face showed strength mixed with intelligence. An ivory-handled Remington Army revolver rode in a cross-draw holster on the left side of his belt and a sheriff's star glinted on his vest.

"Something bothering Olaf, Vandor?" the sheriff inquired, looking at the four men.

At the sight of the peace officer, the giant halted and the other three allowed their hands to relax at their sides. The handsome man moved forward and pointed at the line of horses.

"Them two brought in what looks like Otón Ruiz's *sabino*, Sheriff. We was wondering, natural enough, where they'd got it. Only he got lippy when we asked."

"I'm a mite choosey how I get asked," the Kid put in.

"Then I'll ask you," the sheriff said quietly, right hand resting on the center of his gunbelt.

"We found the hosses straying, back along the stage-trail," lied the Kid. "Brought them in to tell you about them and let you handle things, Sheriff."

Everything about Day Leckenby impressed the Kid with his honesty and capability. There had been neither suspicion nor bluster in his words, but they had held a warning that he intended to have his question answered. The Kid preferred that the sheriff be alone before hearing the truth.

"Do you have business in town?" Leckenby asked, in the neutral voice of a peace officer addressing a potential source of trouble.

"Not me," the Kid replied, without looking at the quartet. "Miss Canary here, though, she's got——"

"*Canary!*" the smallest of the gunslingers burst out, before a glare from Vandor stopped him.

"Martha Jane Canary, mister," Calamity told him. "I've come up to take a look at the Rafter C."

Watching the quartet, the Kid saw the glances which bounced back and forward between three of them. The bald giant stood as if turned to stone, showing no interest in what went on. When one of his companions seemed about to speak, Vandor gave a savage shake of his head and the man kept silent.

"Let's go back and leave the sheriff tend to things, boys," Vandor said. "That's what he's paid for. Ruiz and Job Hogue quit working for the boss a fair piece back. It ain't likely they'd still be around here."

Turning, the three men were about to walk about. Olaf never moved, but stood staring with unwinking eyes at the Kid. Not until Vandor spoke, telling him to come, did the giant turn and follow his companions.

"That was a mean-looking cuss," Calamity breathed, following the Kid into the sheriff's office.

"I've asked Miss Eastfield to keep him out of town," Leckenby replied, closing the door and indicating the chairs at one side of his desk. While his visitors sat down, he walked to the other side. "She reckons he's harmless as long as nobody bothers him. He is, as long as her or Vandor's around to keep him that way."

"Feller wasn't doing his work too good," the Kid said quietly. "One more step 'n' I'd've stopped him."

"So you're Howie Canary's lil gal from back East," Leckenby remarked, letting the Kid's comment go by and sitting down.

"I don't reckon pappy knowed where I was at. He wasn't much for writing home, even if we'd've been there to get letters. Folks got to calling me 'Calamity Jane' that much I sorta of stopped using my real name."

"Calamity Jane, huh. You drive for Alvin Killem, don't you?"

"Dunno about the 'Alvin' part, Sheriff," Calamity grinned. "Most folks call him 'Dobe,' 'cause he don't cotton to them saying 'Cecil.' "

"Is that ole Dobe's for-real name?" the Kid asked.

"Yep," the girl confirmed. "Only don't you let him know I told you."

"I know Calamity's name, Texas," the sheriff hinted, satisfied by her knowledge that she worked for Dobe Killem.

"Loncey Dalton Ysabel," the Kid supplied.

"Known as the Ysabel Kid?" Leckenby asked.

"Among other things," Calamity sniffed.

"We might's well tell you the truth, Sheriff," the Kid said, pulling the kepi down over the girl's eyes. "We didn't exactly find them hosses straying."

"How did you come by 'em?"

"We killed the two fellers who owned them."

Hooking his right boot on to the desk top, Leckenby gazed for a moment at the two young faces. Then he suggested, "Maybe you'd best do some explaining."

"They'd tried to kill Calam twice in Mulrooney, set Spatz's bunch on to us down by the Sappa, then come back in the night to have another go. By that time, I sort of figured they should be discouraged afore they got two real nice folks hurt."

"I'm still listening," Leckenby prompted.

Starting with her reason for being in Mulrooney, Calamity told about the two attempts on her life and the theft of her credentials. Then the Kid took up the story and held nothing back, not even the fact that they had laid a trap for the two men.

"You'd got a good reason," Leckenby ruled, after the Kid had explained why they had made the decision. "Mind if I see them papers, Miss Canary?"

In addition to her own documents, Calamity handed over a letter which Lawyer Talbot had written before they left Mulrooney. It told how she had been robbed, but that Talbot was satisfied with her identity. Returning the papers, the sheriff seemed on the verge of asking a question. Apparently he decided against it, for he let out a chuckle.

"I mind how your pappy got the Rafter C, Calamity. Howie come to town with nothing but a hundred and fifty dollars' worth of wolf-skins. Got the money for 'em and started gambling. He hit the damnedest streak of luck I've ever seen. Couldn't put a foot wrong. Wound up in a poker game with some fellers, including old Coltsal's owned the spread. Coltsal was fixing to sell out 'n' retire and put up the deeds against five thousand dollars on what he figured to be a winning hand. Only it warn't. Not that he was bothered, he'd enough money to last him the rest of his days."

"What happened to Paw after he'd won the game?" Calamity asked.

"He got word of a gold-strike some place and lit out to stake him a claim on it. Before he went, he had the title to the spread turned over in your name so's he wouldn't lose it same way's he got it," Leckenby replied, then after a slight pause, went on, "What're you fixing to do with it?"

"Could be those two *hombres*'d been hired to decide that for her," the Kid put in.

"How'd you mean?" Leckenby asked.

"Getting her killed 'n' stealing her papers'd be a good way of stopping her taking over the spread."

"And?"

"Them folks living out there'd strike some's having a real good reason for wanting that."

"Not Cash Trinian!" Leckenby barked, starting to rise angrily.

"Don't let him rawhide you, Sheriff," Calamity said with a grin. "He don't mean half he says and the other half's not worth listening to."

"Cash Trinian's my friend," the sheriff growled, sitting down.

"How about that Eastfield gal?" Calamity asked. "Seems like them two jaspers used to work for her."

"And them fellers outside looked like they'd heard tell of Martha Jane Canary when we let her name slip out accidental-like," the Kid continued. "What do you know about her, Sheriff?"

"Not a whole heap," the sheriff admitted. "She's had a sawmill built in the hills on the Loup. It's in the county, but I've never had call to go out there."

"You don't like her," the Kid guessed.

"I won't play poker with you," Leckenby grinned. "Nope, I can't say's I'm took with her. There's an owning-look in her eyes, like anything she don't own, she intends to eventual. Could be my imagination."

"Corey-Mae told me that Eastfield wants to buy the Rafter C," Calamity told the peace officer. "And, afore you ask, she don't know I'm who I am."

"That was my idea," the Kid went on. "Those two *hombres* was bringing Calam's papers to somebody up here and I figured it'd be safer not to say who she is until we knowed for sure who was sat where in the game."

"Nobody can blame you for that," Leckenby replied. "What're you figuring on doing now, Calam?"

"Do you want for us to do something special?" the girl asked.

"Stay around town until morning," the sheriff replied. "I believe you, but I aim to telegraph Marshal Beauregard and ask about it. My star's one of the things Miss Eastfield's got her owning look on and I don't aim to give her any chance to get it by reckoning I'm not handling my work right."

"We'll play it your way," the Kid stated and Calamity nodded agreement. "We can go and see Lawyer Endicott tonight and save time, Calam."

"Spend the night at my house, if you like," the

sheriff offered. "Millie 'n' me like company. You can put up your hosses at my barn."

"That's good of you," Calamity smiled.

"Smart, too," grinned Leckenby. "Then I can say, if anybody asks, I'm holding on to you until I've checked out what you've told me about the two hosses you found straying."

Coming to his feet, Leckenby led the way to the door. He opened it and let the other two out ahead of him. On the sidewalk, the Kid came to a halt and looked across the street.

"That's Miss Eastfield," the sheriff said, following the direction of the Kid's gaze.

"Figures," the Texan answered, swinging up his Winchester to rest its barrel on his right shoulder, "company she's keeping."

Calamity studied the woman who was walking across the street followed by the four men. About thirty-five years of age, she had a buxom, medium-sized figure that looked firm and hard, not fat. Two bunches of blonde hair showed from under the Stetson on her head. Her face was good-looking, if not beautiful, but had a hard set to its features. She wore a white shirt-waist, black bolero jacket, doeskin divided skirt and calf-long riding boots.

"Mr. Vandor tells me that you're Miss Canary," the blonde said, coming to a halt without mounting the sidewalk. "You don't look like an Eastern girl."

"Other folks've maybe made the same mistake," Calamity answered.

"I'm Florence Eastfield. Can we talk?"

"I've heard you and I know I can. Go to it."

"In private," Florence suggested. "Perhaps in my buggy, over there?"

"Here's private enough for me," Calamity answered, glancing at the buggy and the four horses from out front of the Clipper saloon at the other side of the street. "Unless you'd like to come 'round some time tomorrow."

"I have to go back to my sawmill tonight," Florence gritted. Clearly she was not used to having people go against her wishes. "And my business with you is confidential."

"Meaning I'd spread it around, Miss Eastfield?" Leckenby inquired mildly.

"Put any meaning you want to it, Sheriff," Florence answered, darting a glance in the Kid's direction. Her eyes were cold, hard, warning that she was used to having her own way.

"Maybe I'm not thinking of selling the Rafter C," Calamity said.

"I can up any offer Tr—you're made for it," Florence answered, jerking her gaze back to the girl.

"Happen I want to sell, I'll keep it in mind," Calamity promised.

"Miss Canary!" Florence barked as the girl started to turn away. "I always get anything I set my heart on."

"That's a good habit," Calamity answered. "I'm near on the same. I don't let *anybody* take something that I want."

"You want for me to stop her disrespecting you, Flo?" rumbled Olaf.

"Keep him back!" Leckenby ordered.

"Or?" Florence challenged.

Like a flash the Kid's rifle swung its barrel downward and the foregrip slapped into the palm of his left hand. Held waist high, it pointed its muzzle directly at the giant's head.

"If the sheriff don't stop him, I will," the dark young Texan promised.

"Stand still, Olaf," Florence said and the man halted as if he had walked into a wall. "Are you standing for this, Sheriff?"

"Nope," Leckenby replied. "That's why I told you to keep him back."

"This makes five times you've taken sides against me, Leckenby!" Florence hissed. "I'm getting tired of it."

"You call it taking sides. I say I'm stopping your men making trouble," the sheriff corrected, right hand pointing toward the Remington's butt. "And it'll be six, happen Torp don't quick move his hand."

Giving a guilty start, the smallest of the gunslingers let fall away the hand that had been creeping toward his gun.

"That's better," the Kid drawled. "You near on

got a rifle ball in the head, *hombre,* 'n' should thank the sheriff polite for saving you."

"So, Miss Canary," Florence purred. "You've brought in a hired gun to help you hang on to your property."

"You want my ranch bad?" Calamity asked, facing the woman.

"I intend to have it!"

"All right, then. I'll go get the deeds from the law-wrangler right now. Then you 'n' me'll go around to the Wells Fargo corral. Just us. Not my hired gun, nor your'n. And you can have them deeds—if you can take 'em offen me."

A small crowd had gathered, hovering in the background and taking in every word. Calamity's suggestion brought a muted, but still audible rumble of excited and anticipatory comment from the audience. For a moment Calamity thought that Florence aimed to take up the challenge. Clenching her fists, the blonde studied Calamity with hate-filled eyes. Then, slowly, Florence let her hands drop to her sides.

"I'm a businesswoman, not some cat-house tail-peddler," the blonde sniffed. "I'll give you——"

"I've told you the price for my ranch," Calamity cut in flatly. "That you, just you, take it off me."

Again talk welled up among the onlookers. Swinging around, Florence glared at the assembled people. When she swung back toward the trio on the sidewalk, her face showed rage and determination.

"You've had my last offer, Canary," the blonde declared. "And you, Leckenby, this county's not big enough to hold me and anybody who's against me."

"Was that what you sent Otón 'n' Job to tell me?" Calamity inquired.

"I've no idea what you're talking about," Florence spat and spun on her heel. "Let's go, men."

"I'm right sorry to've brought fuss on you, Sheriff," Calamity said, watching Florence board the buggy and drive off accompanied by the four men.

"It'd've come sooner or later," Leckenby replied, holding his voice down so that the words would not reach the crowd. "When she says I'm again' her, she's close to being right."

"A man like you'd have to have a better reason than just friendship for taking sides," the Kid commented.

"I figure I've got 'em," Leckenby answered, pleasure at the compliment mingling with the sober gravity on his face. "Soon after they got here, I met up with the boss of the crew's built the sawmill. He was a drinking man's liked to talk; which I've allus been a good listener, especially when it's something's affects my county. He told me's how the Eastfield family'd got a real big contract to cut timber and deliver it to Burwell."

"There's plenty of timber on the hills," drawled the Kid. "And it'd bring money into the county."

"Did you ever see a hill range after all its timber'd been cut?" the sheriff asked, leading Calamity and the Kid along the sidewalk and watching the crowd disperse.

"Can't say I have," the Kid admitted and Calamity shook her head.

"It's ruined," Leckenby stated vehemently. "With all the big trees gone, there's nothing to shelter what small stuff the loggers haven't bust down or trampled underfoot. So it dies off. Then the rains wash away the soil, 'cause there's nothing to hold it. That makes the rivers 'n' streams into mudholes that fish can't live in nor cattle drink out of. I've seen it happen, Kid, Calamity. That's what she'll bring here, unless she's stopped."

"Is it that bad?" Calamity asked.

"It is," Leckenby replied. "To fill her contract, she won't leave a tree standing the length of those hills."

"With something like that on hand," drawled the Kid, "why in hell does she want Calamity's land?"

"I don't know," the sheriff answered. "Maybe Orde Endicott can tell you. Only we'll get you settled in at my place afore we go to see him."

Chapter 12

OLAF'LL BREAK HIM IN TWO

~ ~

BEING MARRIED TO A PEACE OFFICER FOR SEVERAL years had accustomed Millie Leckenby to surprises. So the plump, cheerful-looking woman showed no concern at learning she would have two visitors for the night. She did not even seem put out at the sight of Calamity's unconventional attire. There was only one spare room at the small house, but the Kid said that he would be all right in the stable. While hospitable, Mrs. Leckenby did not look as if she would condone bundling, even with the use of a virtue-saving pine-board. Telling the sheriff to help the youngsters stable their horses, she went to make up a bed for Calamity.

"Florence Eastfield's face when you offered to

fight her for the deeds," Leckenby chuckled, as they walked inside the barn. "What'd you've done if she'd called your bluff?"

"I wasn't bluffing," Calamity replied calmly. "Shucks, I one time licked a gal's claimed to be the female fist-fighting champeen of the world."*

"How'd you do that?" the sheriff asked, still grinning.

"Got her fighting *my* way, 'stead of her'n," Calamity explained. "And I'd got me a shy lil schoolmarm from back East helping me."

Before the girl could go into greater detail, a gangling, excited-looking townsman appeared at the stable door.

"Day!" he said. "It's old Skelter. He's got this scattergun and's headed for the Fittern place."

"Damn it!" the sheriff snorted and looked at his guests. "Sorry, Calam, Kid. This's an old fuss. I'll have to ride out there and quieten things down."

"Need any help?" asked the Kid.

"Nope," Leckenby replied. "I'll take ole Buck there and handle it on my own."

Figuring that the sheriff was the best judge of the matter, the Kid did not press his offer. Courtesy had required that he make it, but he did not wish to leave Calamity unescorted in the town.

While the sheriff saddled his big buckskin, Calamity and the Kid attended to their horses.

---

* Told in *Trouble Trail*.

Night had fallen by the time they went up to the house and told Mrs. Leckenby of her husband's departure. The woman heard the news with no sign of alarm. It was, she explained, not an unusual occurrence for the sheriff to have to quieten down either Skelter or Fittern. A pair of irascible old-timers, they carried on a long-standing feud. Mostly it simmered harmlessly, being continued, Mrs. Leckenby suspected, as a means of avoiding boredom. On the rare occasions when tempers rose too high, the sheriff was needed to apply a restraining influence.

"It'll take Day about two hours to get out there and back," Mrs. Leckenby finished. "We'll wait supper for him, unless you're hungry."

"Ate right well with Corey-Mae and Cash Trinian," Calamity told her. "What say we go see Lawyer Endicott right now, Lon?"

"Not until you've had a cup of coffee," the sheriff's wife stated. "It's all ready for you."

After drinking their coffee, Calamity and the Kid rose to leave. They had placed their Winchesters on the wall-rack and left them there. Mrs. Leckenby told them how to locate Endicott's home and asked that they should bring the lawyer back with them. Agreeing to do so, Calamity requested that the woman keep her documents. Florence Eastfield and her men had left town, but there was no point in taking needless chances. Mrs. Leckenby accepted the envelope and locked it in the drawer of her husband's desk.

Although Calamity and the Kid found the main street deserted on their return, they did not feel surprised. It was Thursday and in the middle of the month, so the town would not be over lively. Going between two buildings, they followed Mrs. Leckenby's directions. By the livery barn, they located Endicott's house. It did not strike them as the dwelling to be expected as a successful lawyer's residence. The whole place was in darkness, which did not hide its tumble-down aspect.

"He ain't to home," called a voice from by the barn.

"Where's he at, then?" asked the Kid, turning to face the speaker.

"Down at the Clipper," the man answered. "Where else? Damned drunk."

"Let's go get him," Calamity suggested and made a wry face. "From the look of this place and the way that feller talks, I can see why the pride of that fancy Eastern law school wound up here."

Returning to the main street, they headed toward the Clipper Saloon. Its hitching rail was devoid of horses and trade seemed to be very bad, if the lack of noise from inside was anything to go on. Two boys stood on the seat, looking over the painted lower section of the left side's window. Hearing Calamity and the Kid approaching, they turned.

"What's up?" the girl asked tolerantly.

"They're getting old Lawyer Endicott liquored

up in there," one of the boys replied. "He's a screaming whoop when he's that ways, until he falls asleep that is."

Being aware that baiting a drunkard, especially if he also happened to be well-educated, was a favorite indoor sport of small-town loafers, Calamity let out an explosive snort and headed for the batwing doors. A good-hearted girl, she hated petty cruelty of that kind. Even without having need of the lawyer's professional services she would have reacted in the same manner. Slipping her whip from its loop, she went striding into the Clipper Saloon.

Knowing his Calamity, the Kid followed on her heels. He reckoned that she might require some backing if the men concerned with the lawyer-baiting objected to her intervention. Just a moment too late, as the doors swung closed behind them, the Kid realized that they had walked into a trap.

The barman stood behind the counter, looking scared. Off to the right of the room, Olaf was seated facing a tall, thin, unshaven man wearing a threadbare, but once expensive suit, a grubby, collarless white shirt and scuffed, cracked town boots. Two grimy hands gripped at a beer schooner into which the giant was pouring the contents of a whiskey bottle. The long-handled axe lay across the table.

Even as a realization of the danger bit at the Kid, he heard a footfall from behind him and felt the hard muzzle of a revolver gouge into his back. At the same moment, a muffled curse from Calamity caused the Kid to turn his head. The smallest of the three gunslingers they had last seen with Florence Eastfield stood behind the girl. He had his arms locked tight about her elbows and torso, and knew enough to keep his face clear of her head.

"Unbuckle the gunbelt, cow-nurse!" ordered Vandor's voice from beyond the revolver. "And don't you make fuss, gal, or he's dead."

Calamity knew when to surrender. So she stopped struggling; but still retained her hold of the whip. Equally aware of the futility of resisting at that moment, the Kid slowly obeyed the order. Unbuckling his gunbelt, he let it slide to his feet. Vandor placed his left palm against the center of the black shirt and pushed the Kid forward.

"What's on your mind, *hombre*?" the Kid inquired.

"You disrespected Miss Eastfield out there in the street, while you was stood behind a rifle and backed by Leckenby," Vandor explained, following him and thrusting him farther from the door. "Olaf didn't like it. Did you, Olaf?"

Turning his head slowly, the giant hurled the empty bottle across the room. He lurched to his feet, ignoring the lawyer who sat drinking from the schooner.

"Olaf didn't like it!" the giant rumbled. "Olaf'll break him in two."

"You standing for this, barkeep?" asked the Kid, watching the giant. "I don't reckon the sheriff'll be too happy if you do."

"Maybe Leckenby won't be coming back," Vandor sneered, retreating toward the door. "And if he don't, Miss Eastfield'll want to know who her friends are. Take him, Olaf!"

Letting out a bellow more animal than human, the giant lurched in the Kid's direction. At the table, Endicott set down the glass and stared through bleary eyes at the big man.

"Wha-Wha——!" the lawyer mumbled. "Dish-grashe-ful be-hav-hav——" He took up the schooner again and drank deeply.

Separated from his weapons, the Kid was far from helpless. Although the Comanches preferred more direct, permanent methods of settling quarrels, they knew some effective bare-hand fighting tricks. In addition, the Kid had watched such masters as Dusty Fog and Mark Counter perform, learning valuable lessons from them. So he reckoned that he would not be the easy victim the men—and maybe Calamity—expected.

Gripping the back of a chair, the Kid leaped to meet the advancing giant. At the last moment, the Kid weaved aside and crashed his weapon into Olaf's chest. Wood splintered and the chair disintegrated in the Kid's hands. Apart from a single grunt, the giant gave no sign of feeling a blow that would have felled most men. As the Kid started to go by, Olaf swung his left arm. It caught the Texan a glancing blow on the shoulder. Glancing, maybe, but the force of it sent the Kid staggering across the room.

"That does it!" Vandor said enthusiastically, watching the Kid's attack. "There'll be no stopping that crazy bongo until he's killed the Texan. Hold on to the gal, Torp. I'll go fetch the hosses."

"Sure, Van," the other man replied, tightening his grip on Calamity. "I'll stop in here 'til you get back. I'm enjoying this."

"Want to bet you stay that way, you stinking son-of-a-bitch?" Calamity thought, her eyes on the fight.

With surprising speed, the bald man turned and charged after the Kid. Managing to turn, the Texan struck with his back against the wall. Pinned there momentarily, he saw Olaf coming closer. When in range, the man launched up his right leg in a kick. Crossing his wrists, the Kid interposed them between his body and the rising leg. Even with the support offered by the X-block he had learned from Dusty Fog, he only just halted the boot clear of him. Changing his hand position fast, he gripped the raised ankle in them. Then he leaped to one side and gave the trapped limb a savage lateral swing. For a moment Olaf's other spiked boot held on to the planks beneath it. Then it slipped and he spun around, away from the Texan. Following the staggering man, the Kid interlaced his fingers and smashed his hands as hard as he could against the base of Olaf's spine. Again the giant grunted, stumbling but not going down.

Going after the giant, the Kid learned the advantage offered by the caulked boots. Ramming down his forward foot, Olaf halted. He pivoted around, swinging his right fist. Desperately the Kid tried to twist aside. The back of the forearm crashed into his chest and the force of the blow pitched him backward. Hitting a table, he went over it and landed on the floor. Dazed and winded, he saw Olaf stalking with measured strides toward him. Taking hold of the table in both hands, the man swung it above his head as if it weighed no more than a matchstick.

Down drove the table. Throwing himself over, the Kid just managed to roll clear. He heard the table drive edge-first into the floor and shatter, continuing to roll. With a bestial snarl, Olaf flung away the ruins of the table and stalked after the Texan.

At the door, Calamity watched the fight with worried eyes. She knew that she could not break Torp's hold on her by sheer strength. However, as the fight progressed, his attention became absorbed by it. That was what the girl had been hoping for. Feeling his grip slacken a little, she raised her right foot and stamped it down hard on to Torp's left instep. Worn for utility rather than feminine fashion, Calamity's footwear was solidly constructed. So the force of her attack drove pain through her captor's foot and leg. Torp let out a howl and his arms loosened their hold.

Not much, but enough. Drawing forward, Calamity propelled the handle of her whip to the rear. The hard knob of the butt rammed into Torp's solar plexus. Belching out a gasp of agony, he released her entirely and started to go backward. Calamity swung around and lashed out with her whip-filled right hand. The back of her fist caught Torp at the side of the head. Spinning in a circle, he blundered into the batwing doors and passed through. Still unable to halt himself, he crossed the sidewalk, collided with the hitching rail's end-post and tumbled on to his hands and knees in the street.

On the point of following Torp and making sure he could not return, Calamity heard the crash of the table. Turning her head, she saw that the Kid needed help in the worst kind of way. Three strides across the room carried Calamity close enough to give it. Already her right arm had sent the whip's lash curling behind her. Forward the arm snapped and the lash reversed its direction.

Looking up, the Kid saw Olaf's right foot raised and poised to crash the sharp spikes into him. If he could only have a moment to catch his breath, he might yet escape. The moment was to be granted to him. Something brown wrapped itself around the man's head. Still standing on one leg, Olaf screamed in agony as the whip's lash bit into his face. Calamity tugged back on the handle, pulling the man off balance. Although he sent the boot driving down, he just missed the Kid. Up rose Olaf's hands, tearing the lash from his face and flinging it aside. Then he started to rush across the room.

Seeing in which direction the giant was headed. Calamity dropped her whip and reached for her Navy Colt. Then she heard the rumble of hooves and voices raised in the street. Realizing that the sounds heralded Vandor's return, and noticing that the Kid was already on his hands and knees as he started to get up, she knew that she must try to prevent the gunslingers from coming back into the barroom. Backing hurriedly toward the doors, she hooked her left boot under the Kid's gunbelt and sent it skidding across the floor in his direction.

"Lon!" she yelled, drawing his attention from the bald giant and to the belt which halted several feet from the Texan.

Sweeping Endicott aside as he tried to rise, Olaf snatched up the axe. Mouthing barely human sounds, the giant turned and rushed toward the Kid. Still only half erect, the Texan saw the man approaching. Around whistled the axe, swung with the speed, power and precision of a trained lumberjack. The Kid propelled himself toward his gunbelt, barely passing clear of the axe's swinging arc. Diving, the Texan extended his right hand as he landed belly-down on the floor. His fingers closed about the butt and he plucked the old Dragoon from its holster. Nearer came the giant's feet, sounding and vibrating through the planks. Twisting on to his back, the Kid saw Olaf looming toward him and the axe swinging into the air. Thrusting the Dragoon upward, the Kid drew its trigger to the rear with his right forefinger as the heel of his left hand flashed over to drive back and release the hammer.

Fanning a single-action revolver, which had to be cocked between each shot, was the fastest known way of turning lead loose. It was also a measure of desperation, especially when using the four-pound-one-ounce, thumb-busting old Dragoon Colt. Twice the Kid slapped back the hammer, riding the wicked recoil between the shots. Both bullets lanced into Olaf's torso, but even then, if he had been using a lesser weapon, the Kid might not have saved his life. Each chamber of the revolver held forty grains of powder, almost twice the charge used in a Winchester *rifle*. That gave the Dragoon a power which would not be equaled in a handgun until superior steel and smokeless powder brought the mighty .44 Magnum cartridge into being.

Two 219-grain bullets, traveling at around 900 feet-per-second, were more than even Olaf's giant frame could absorb and remain standing. Instead of completing his blow, he pitched over backward and the axe dropped from his hands. Olaf was dead before he hit the floor. Across the room Endicott lay crumpled against the front of the bar.

At the door, Calamity flattened herself against the wall and looked out. Vandor sat his horse, leading three others, in the center of the street. Suddenly, as the Kid's Dragoon began to crash behind her, Calamity saw Vandor rein in the horses. Torp was lurching toward him, pointing toward the saloon and speaking, but Vandor hardly looked his way.

"It's the sheriff!" the handsome gunslinger growled, indicating something beyond Calamity's range of vision. "Poole must've missed him. Get the hell out of here, Torp!"

"What's happening, Calam?" the Kid asked, forcing himself erect and moving toward her.

"It's them two gun-slicks," the girl replied, then hooves rumbled and moved away. "They looked like they was fixing to come busting in here. Only Vandor yelled something about the sheriff and they lit out like the devil after a yearling."

Thrusting through the doors, the Kid lunged across the sidewalk and landed on the street. He saw the two men disappearing at a gallop into an alley farther down and across the street. As they went out of sight before he could raise the Dragoon, he looked for the reason behind their departure. Hearing another set of hooves in the opposite direction to that taken by the hired guns, he swung toward the sound. Patches of light scattered along the street, from the illuminated windows of various business premises. A big light-colored horse walked into one of them.

Instantly the Kid knew that something was wrong. He identified the horse as Leckenby's buckskin. While the sheriff was on its back, he was not behaving in a natural manner. Instead of urging his horse to a better pace and holding a gun as he came to investigate, he sat stiff in his saddle with the animal moving at a steady walk. Even as the Kid looked, the buckskin turned and continued at the same pace into an alley.

"Calam!" the Kid barked, ignoring the people who began to congregate. "Let's go, *pronto*!"

Having seen that there was no chance of taking up matters with the gunslingers, Calamity had holstered her Colt, then returned to collect her whip and the Kid's gunbelt. With the belt hanging over her left shoulder and coiling the whip, she joined the Kid in the street.

"What's up?" she asked.

"I reckon the sheriff's been hurt," the Kid replied. "We'd best——"

"What's happened in there?" asked a tall, lean man in town clothes and carrying a doctor's bag. He was in the front of the crowd, along with half a dozen men who looked like they had been a long time west of the Mississippi, even if they had lived in towns rather than on the range.

"Vandor set Olaf on the Texan," the bartender replied, coming through the batwing doors.

"Seeing's you're here," the spokesman spoke dryly to the Kid, "I'd say Olaf's dead. I'm not surprised——"

"Are you a doctor?" interrupted the Kid.

"If I'm not, young feller, there's a lot of people around here should have worries," the man answered. "Who's hurt in there?"

"Nobody's you can fix," growled the Kid. "I reckon the sheriff's been shot!"

Talk rumbled up and, watching the faces around him, the Kid saw mixed emotions. Some of the people looked surprised, others appeared to be worried and cast anxious glances around them. The six men hovering behind the doctor reacted as the Kid had expected they would. All showed interest, concern, but not fear for their own safety. The doctor proved to be a man of action.

"Let's go!" he snapped. "I don't need a crowd to watch me work. Some of you help Sid to clear up in there. Harry, you and the boys head for home then meet me at Day's house."

"We'll do that," declared a gnarled old-timer among the six.

On joining the Kid, Calamity had returned her whip to its loop and taken his Dragoon, leaving him free to retrieve and buckle on his gunbelt. Returning the old gun to leather, he went with the girl and the doctor along the street. Taking the lead, the medical man swung down an alley. While walking, the Kid told of his suspicions and found that the doctor agreed with him.

"You're right. Day'd've come barreling down that street, gun out and ready to use it if he'd been all right."

At that moment they came into sight of the sheriff's house and any hopes they cherished that the Kid might be wrong were wiped away by what they saw. Leckenby's big buckskin stood at the picket fence's gate and the house's front door was open. Staggering under his weight, Mrs. Leckenby was helping her husband along the path. She looked around as she heard the running feet. Coming up fast, Calamity and the two men closed around the couple. Although hit high up in the right side of his chest and with his shirt soaked by blood, the sheriff was still conscious.

"It—It's come—Doc!" Leckenby gasped. "Got me—Buck—carried me clear. Sen-Send—for Cash—Trini——"

The words ended and the sheriff went limp in the men's arms.

Chapter 13

NOBODY LIKES HANGINGS

~~~~

"WHERE'S THE KID?" MRS. LECKENBY ASKED, coming from the bedroom into which, half an hour before, her husband had been carried.

"Some fellers come, toting shotguns 'n' painted for war," Calamity answered, drawing out a chair and seating the haggard-faced woman in it. "He's got two of 'em watching front 'n' back 'n's took the other two into town to help ask questions." She indicated the coffee-pot and other utensils on the table. "I hope you don't mind, but I threw up some coffee for us."

"Thank you, Calamity."

"How's the sheriff?"

"The doctor's still working on him."

"Looks like he knows what he's doing."

"Manny's good at his work," Mrs. Leckenby confirmed. "Did you see Orde Endicott, Calamity?"

Knowing that the question had come out of a desire to avoid thinking about her own troubles, Calamity told the woman what had happened. When the girl concluded her story with a blistering condemnation of the lawyer, Mrs. Leckenby shook her head.

"He's got cause for being what he is, Calamity. You said that you'd heard he was a good lawyer. He was, a great one."

"He sure ain't now!" Calamity growled, pouring out cups of coffee.

"No, not now," Mrs. Leckenby conceded. "He used to be and had a fine future ahead of him, as a defense attorney back East. He was against hanging."

"Nobody likes hangings, but there's times when they're necessary."

"He didn't think so and always claimed hanging didn't stop people committing murders."

"*Maybe* they don't stop 'em," Calamity grunted. "But they sure make folks think twice afore murdering or stealing hosses. And hanging stops 'em doing it twice."

"Orde Endicott learned *that,* the hard way," Mrs. Leckenby said gently. "He was so obsessed with the idea that he took up the case of a man, a butler, found guilty of the brutal murder of a woman. Although Orde knew the man was guilty, he obtained a retrial. At that time he had the political connections to do it."

"What'd he do a fool thing like that for?"

"It was his belief that if he could make people think an innocent man had nearly been hung, there would be a public outcry to stop all hanging. In the retrial, he pulled every trick he knew—confused the witnesses, brought up misleading points and pieces of false evidence. He even had a false confession obtained from a dying criminal——"

"The lousy son-of-a-bitch!" Calamity spat out.

"He thought he was acting for the best," Mrs. Leckenby answered gently. "And he paid a high price for it. The man was acquitted and set free. To show his faith in him, Orde hired him as his butler. It was a gesture designed to prove that even a guilty man could redeem himself given the chance—and it failed."

"How come?"

"Less than a month later the man killed two more women in the same drugged rage that had caused his first victim's death. He smoked marijuana cigarettes, which Orde had insisted were harmless. One of the victims was Orde's wife."

"The hell you say!" Calamity breathed. "So that's why he moved West for his health."

"That's why," the woman agreed. "He nearly went off his head. His health was ruined and he

took to drinking. Naturally, all his influential political friends deserted him. They were a pack of
liberal-intellectual scum who didn't dare face up to
the public outcry. Orde drifted around, until we
found him and brought him here."

"You?" Calamity asked.

"I'm his sister," the woman said simply. "We
fetched him to Hollick City, got him sober enough
to hang out his shingle and do what little legal
work's needed here. There's not a lot and he can
handle it well enough, when he's sober."

"I'm sorry I called him what I did," Calamity
said contritely.

"He was misguidedly stupid," the sheriff's wife
answered. "But he paid for——"

A knock at the front door ended the words and
brought both women to their feet. The Kid entered, crossing to the table and laying his rifle on
it. Before leaving, he had collected the weapon
from the rack.

"I found the feller's told the sheriff about that
fuss," he said. "He was scared white-haired."

"Afore, or after, you found him?" Calamity
asked dryly.

"Both. Seems like that Vandor *hombre* told him
about seeing Old Man Skelter toting the scatter toward the Fittern place and he just brought the
word out of civic duty."

"Does the feller still have his ears?" Calamity inquired.

"Just about. I stopped them two gents I was with tearing 'em off," the Kid replied. "Town's about even in its feelings, ma'am. But most of 'em're set to back up your husband, well or hurt."

"I knew they would," Mrs. Leckenby sighed, eyes bright. At such a time, a local peace officer learned how his town regarded him. It seemed that the majority of Hollick City's population respected her husband sufficiently to stand by him. Then she saw the misery on the girl's face and asked, "What is it, Calamity?"

"I feel that I brought all this on, coming here!" Calamity answered.

"Like the sheriff said on the street," drawled the Kid. "It'd've come sooner or later. You arriving likely brought it to the boil."

"Neither I nor Day blame you for coming, child," Mrs. Leckenby went on. "We've been expecting trouble from that Eastfield woman for a long time."

"They'd never've dast make that play again' us with the sheriff around," the Kid stated. "So they lured him out of town and bushwhacked him. Ma'am, I'm real sorry. I should've asked when I come in. How is the sheriff?"

"Doctor Goldberg's still with him."

"He'll pull through," the Kid predicted. "And, ma'am, way I see it, your husband's a forty-four-caliber man."

Knowing that such a tribute was high indeed

when given by a Texan,* Mrs. Leckenby showed pleasure despite her worry.

"Way those two polecats lit out when they saw the sheriff coming into town, I'll go along with all Lon's said," Calamity remarked. "They didn't have the guts to face up to your husband and Lon here."

The bedroom door opened and Doctor Goldberg stepped out. Coming to her feet, Mrs. Leckenby needed only to look at his face to know the answer, but she asked the question just the same.

"How is he?"

"Stubborn, ornery, with a body, that I should mention such a thing in front of a young lady, that would stop a cannon-ball," Goldberg answered. "He'll live, but he's off his feet for a spell. I'll ask Hal, or Swede to ride out to the Rafter C for Cash Trinian."

"Best let me go, Doc," the Kid suggested quietly. "Might be they've got somebody watching the trail. If they have, somebody could get hurt."

"You go then," Goldberg confirmed. "I've got enough sick folk on my hands right now and don't want more."

"Don't let that worry you," drawled the Kid mildly. "Happen there's anybody watching the trail, you won't be needed."

"Want me along, Lon?" asked Calamity.

"I can handle it best on my lonesome," the Kid

---

* How the tribute originated is told in *.44 Calibre Man*.

replied. "You stay put, gal. Maybe Miss Eastfield's decided the time's come to stop looking and start owning. Which, she'll likely be coming with help."

"If she does," Calamity gritted. "Could be I'll get her in that corral yet."

"Just do me one lil-bitsy favor, gal," drawled the Kid, taking up his rifle. "Let her come and ask you, don't you go looking for her."

"What do you reckon I am?" Calamity yelled at the Kid's departing back.

Waiting until he had reached and opened the door, the young Texan turned and replied, "That I can't tell you, there's a lady in the room."

Letting out a yelp like a scalded cat, Calamity grabbed for the coffee-pot. Then she remembered where she was, and, anyway, the Kid had already gone through the door. So she gave an exasperated groan.

"Ooh! Them floating-Outfit yahoos're all the same!"

"He gave good advice, young lady," Goldberg pointed out.

"Sure," Calamity grinned. "And, for once just to rile him, I'm going to take it. Have some coffee, Doc."

"Going some place, Kid?" asked a gray-haired member of the quartet seated on the house's front porch and nursing shotguns.

"Got scared, Swede," the Kid replied. "I'm running out."

"Scared of Flo Eastfield's bunch?" asked the portly owner of the local bank.

"Nope, of Calamity," grinned the Kid. "Banged fool she-male, she wants to marry me and just now proposed."

"Marriage's a wonderful thing, I allus say," declared the Wells Fargo agent.

"Then why're you still a bachelor?" Swede demanded.

" 'Cause I never believe in doing nothing I ain't done once afore," the agent explained. "Where you headed, Kid?"

"To tell Cash Trinian what's happened," the Kid answered and walked across to enter the stable.

Leaning his Winchester against the wall of the stall, he saddled his white stallion. Taking up the rifle and leading out the horse, he decided against using the rest of the relay. If Florence Eastfield did have a man, or men, watching the trail to the Rafter C, he could handle the menace better with only one mount. The white stallion was the best choice for the work ahead.

Once in the saddle, he kept his rifle in his hand and made his way out of town along the stage-trail. The stallion had been hard-pushed since leaving the trail herd and he wanted to conserve its strength. So he stuck to the easier going offered by the trail, instead of cutting across country, relying upon his and the horse's keen senses to detect hostile presences. Nor did he make the white go at faster than a good trot. Unless Florence East-field had more men on hand—and the way she had handled things led him to believe she had not—she would have to either send for or fetch reinforcements from the sawmill. That meant there would be no further assault on the town before daylight. So he had time to reach the ranch and return with Trinian without causing the stallion to exhaust itself.

The Kid approached the point where the track turned off the main trail without incident. Suddenly, about seventy yards from the old cotton-wood tree, the stallion came to a halt and snorted. Knowing the sound to be that caused by the detection of a hidden human being, the Kid started to raise his rifle. Yet he felt certain that he had heard an animal's low growl just as the horse gave its warning. There had been a bluetick hound capable of making the sound at the Trinian's ranch-house.

"Rafter C!" called the Texan. "This's the Ysabel Kid coming with a message from Millie 'n' Day Leckenby."

"Ride up here slow 'n' easy, young feller," answered a cracked, ancient voice from behind the tree.

"I'll do just that," promised the Kid and, at his signal, the stallion started moving once more.

Cradling his old Spencer carbine ready for use, Leathers of the Rafter C told the bluetick crouched at his side to stay put. Then the old-timer watched the white stallion drawing closer. There was one hell of a fine horse. It moved quietly, despite its size, like a wild mustang rather than a trained saddle-critter. The baby-faced young cowhand had looked to have Indian blood. Horse-Indian most likely. Only a better than fair rider could stay on the stallion's back——

Only the Texan might not be staying on it.

"Hold it right there, feller!" Leathers ordered. "Them black duds make you sort of hard to see."

A low whistle came from the range, sounding uncomfortably like it originated from a position that put Leathers in its maker's view. As the stallion stopped, a quiet, drawling voice rose from the same place.

"Depends on where you're looking."

"Stay put, Sam!" Leathers growled and the dog sank back to the crouching position that it had been on the point of leaving on hearing the Texan's words. "Feller that sneaky's likely to blow your bead off if you start gnawing on his arm."

"Only if he goes higher'n the elbow," the Kid corrected, walking toward the tree. "You out a-courting this late, friend?"

"Courting's for young sprout's hasn't l'arned better sense," Leathers answered, feeling admiration at the way he had been tricked. Concentrating on the approaching stallion, both he and the bluetick had failed to see or hear its rider quit the saddle and take up his present position. "I'm out coon-hunting."

"With *that* relic?" the Kid scoffed, taking his right hand from the rifle to jerk a derisive thumb in the direction of the old-timer's highly prized Spencer. It was also a gesture of peace, for the Kid had removed the hand that would be needed to fire the Winchester.

"When I shoots 'em," Leathers replied, lowering the .52-caliber Spencer, "I aims to see's they stops shot. What's up in town, young feller?"

"Day Leckenby got shot tonight."

"The hell he did! Who done it?"

"One of the sawmill bunch. Sheriff asked for us to come and tell Cash Trinian."

"Figures," Leathers growled. "Cash was a damned good deputy. Get your hoss 'n' ride on, I'll catch up to you along the track. My hoss's hid in a hollow out there."

When Leathers joined him, riding a leggy dun gelding, the Kid explained why he had not come at a faster pace. Then they continued to ride in the direction of the ranch-house. On arrival, they left their horses before the building and went across the front porch. Leathers knocked on the door of the darkened building and, after a moment, a light glowed in one of the windows. Raising the window, Trinian looked out. Telling the men to wait, he disappeared. A minute or so ticked by, then the window went dark and the parlor was illuminated. The door opened and Trinian stood at it, barefoot and with his night-shirt tucked hit-and-miss into his pants. Beyond him, wearing a night-cap and with a robe over her nightgown, Corey-Mae looked worriedly across the room.

"Oh. It's you," Trinian growled ungraciously, letting the Kid and Leathers enter, directing his words at the Texan. "You was a mite cagey last time you called. Didn't hit us until after you'd gone, but Endicott's law-wrangling pard lived in Mulrooney and Calamity Jane 'n' the Canary gal's got one name the same."

"Calam's Martha Jane Canary all right," the Kid admitted. "Only we didn't find them two hosses straying. We'd had to gun down their owners to stop 'em killing us. Thing like that happens, it makes a man careful. And you didn't act any too sociable when we rode up."

"We'd got our reasons——!" Trinian began hotly.

"Why have you come, Kid?" Corey-Mae interrupted.

"Day Leckenby got tricked out of town tonight," the Kid replied. "He was bushwhacked, but got back wounded. It was done so that the Eastfield gal's guns could sic that Olaf *hombre* on to me safe-like."

"Only they didn't sic him on to you, looks like," Trinian growled.

"The hell they didn't!" snapped the Kid, temper starting to rise. "I had to fan two forty-four balls into him to sort of cool him out of the notion. Calamity helped some——"

"What's happened to Day Leckenby?" Corey-Mae cut in. "That's the important thing right now."

"He's hit bad. Sent me to fetch your husband in," the Kid supplied.

"To help him," Trinian demanded, "or you?"

"Cash!" Corey-Mae gasped.

"Him, mister. *Your* friend!" the Kid replied. "I've got all the helping I need on my belt and in my saddle-boot."

"Just a minute, Kid!" Corey-Mae snapped, advancing across the room with bare feet making determined slaps on the floor. "Now both of you stop behaving like stupid boys and start acting like grown men! I'm ashamed of you, Cash Trinian. And you're no better than he is, Lon Ysabel. Sit at that table, both of you!"

There was something commanding and impressive about the way the woman glared at the two abashed men. Under her cold scrutiny, they took seats facing each other across the table. Placing herself in a chair between them, she looked from her husband to the Kid.

"*Men!*" Corey-Mae snorted. "I guessed who Calamity was while we were making the meal. But when the same notion finally struck Cash, he wanted to charge into town for a showdown. I thought that I'd talked him into enough sense to wait until morning and go in to ask what Calamity intends to do with the ranch. One thing I know. Whatever she decides, it will be a fair decision and not based on who rode with what damned stupid outfit in the War."

"You can count on Calam for that, ma'am," the Kid admitted,

"If she was a *man* I'd not be so sure!" Corey-Mae answered, eyeing the men coldly. "Day Leckenby's your friend, Cash. And I'd say you like him, Kid. Even if you don't, it was because of you, and Calamity, that he was shot. But instead of deciding how the hell you can best help him, you're both thinking of who rode in what damned color uniform."

Looking at the Kid, Trinian found the same contrition he himself felt. They each realized that their hostility stemmed from the War rather than any actual difference at that moment.

"You're right, ma'am," the Kid stated. "And I'm sorry for how I behaved under your roof."

"So you should be, making me use cuss-words that way," Corey-Mae smiled. "And Cash is as much to blame as you. When we saw you coming with the *sabino,* he had the kind of idea only a *man* could think up. It was a sneaky play by Eastfield. You'd been sent to sell us the horses cheap, then she could bring up a charge of buying stolen property. That's why we acted the way we did when you arrived."

"I know Calam's got a sneaky, shifty look about her," the Kid grinned. "But everybody with good taste tells me I've got a right honest face. How about it, Cash, are you coming in with me?"

"Yeah——!" Trinian said, starting to rise.

"There you go again!" Corey-Mae sighed. "Cash's been hard at work all day, and you look like you've not slept properly for longer than's good for you, Kid. But you still think you can charge back to town and be of help."

"Well, ma'am——" the Kid began.

"Florence Eastfield had how many men the last time you went up there, Leathers?" Corey-Mae asked.

"Eight at most," the old-timer answered. "So, happen she's not got more in since yesterday, that ain't a whole heap to go up against the town."

"If I know Doc Goldberg and those other hunting and poker-playing reprobates," the woman said, "they'll be around Day Leckenby's house armed to the teeth and all set to lick creation to help him."

"She means the town's leading citizens," Leathers informed the Kid. "I'm one of 'em."

"They're around," the Kid confirmed. "And I reckon Mrs. Trinian called 'em right. You mean there's only eight men at the sawmill?"

"Nary more, not since the fellers who built it for her moved out," Leathers replied. "I'd've expected them to be cutting the timber afore now, but they never got started. 'Cepting that Olaf'd cut some of the stuff close to hand. Must've been trying out the sawmill, or something."

"Then that's settled," Corey-Mae smiled. "You can grab some sleep, both of you, and ride in at sunup. Even then, you'll be there before she can get word to the sawmill and fetch in the rest of her men."

"If eight's all she's got, I don't reckon she'll be back," the Kid decided. "Which, I could stand a night's sleep."

"Then let's chance it," Trinian suggested. "We'll leave here at sunup and should be in well before they couldn've got word to the others at the sawmill and back."

At about eight o'clock the next morning, refreshed by several hours of uninterrupted sleep, the Kid, Trinian and one of the younger hands, a tall, freckled-faced redhead called Staff, rode through Hollick City toward the sheriff's house. Approaching the building, the Kid for one felt sure that something had gone wrong. Several armed townsmen stood around and Swede hurried toward the newcomers.

"Kid!" the man said worriedly. "It's trouble. We found Harry in the stable with a bust head, and Calamity's missing."

"How come?" growled the Kid, and Swede wondered how he had ever thought the Texan looked young or innocent.

"She went down to the stable to see to the hosses just after sunup," the man explained. "We never saw nor heard nothing, and just now Millie asked me to go down and tell her breakfast was waiting. That's when I found Harry and Calam's hat."

"I've sent for hosses," the Wells Fargo agent went on, coming forward. "We was all set to go after her."

"Not you," the Kid answered, silently cursing himself for remaining at the ranch. "They see so many coming, they'll kill Calam for sure. This's a chore for one man. Me."

"Three of us'd be small enough to keep hid," Trinian objected. "And I know the range better'n you. I can take you straight to the sawmill."

"Who's the other?" asked the Kid.

"Staff. He's a good hand with a gun and no heavy-boot comes to quiet moving."

"This's not your fight," the Kid pointed out.

"The hell it's not!" Trinian replied. "You saw Corey-Mae in action last night. Do you reckon I dast go back there and tell her what's happened, unless I'd helped you get that gal back safe and well?"

"Likely you dasn't," admitted the Kid.

"And anyways," Trinian went on. "I don't know what Calamity plans to do with the ranch, but I'd say our chances are a whole heap better with her than if Florence Eastfield comes to own it."

Chapter 14

YOU'D BETTER HOPE THIS WORKS

CALAMITY COULD, AND DID, BITTERLY CURSE HERSELF for getting captured so easily. Seated on the saddle of a strange horse, covered to the waist by an empty grain sack which let in no light, her arms pinioned and feet fastened to the stirrup irons, she had muttered savage invective against her captors and her own stupidity. Yet, she told herself, as the horse and its companions on either side of her came to a halt, it was always easy to be wise after some damned fool thing had happened.

With the Kid seen on his way the previous evening, Calamity had helped Mrs. Leckenby to feed the men who had gathered to protect the sheriff. All sensible precautions had been taken, including a guard being placed in the stable. Sent to collect him, two of the men had carried Lawyer Endicott from the Clipper Saloon. He had been too far gone in a drunken stupor for Calamity to hope to discuss business with him. At first the girl had been a mite alarmed by the Kid's failure to return. Mrs. Leckenby had guessed what was happening and insisted that Calamity go to bed. Being more tired than she cared to admit, the girl had obeyed.

Exhausted and in a safe bed, Calamity did not wake until seven o'clock. Slipping out of bed, she had donned shirt, pants and moccasins, then strapped on her gunbelt with Colt and whip, before going across to the stable to tend to the horses. Putting on her weapons had gained her nothing. As she had walked through the stable's door, the grain sack had descended over her head and shoulders. Before she could struggle or raise the alarm, a hand had clapped over her mouth and a rope secured her arms from outside the sack. One of her assailants had disarmed her, then she had been swung on to a man's shoulder and carried away.

Taken a short distance that way, she had been placed on a horse and lashed afork it. Then her captors, she had guessed at there being only two of them, had led her mount after their own. They had splashed through the Middle Loup River and gone on another couple of miles before coming to a halt.

The man to her right loosened the rope about

the sack, but did not remove her bonds completely. Instead he jerked the sack out from under them. Half-blinded by the sudden flood of light, Calamity was unable to do anything before the rope tightened again. Shaking her head to remove the dizziness she felt, Calamity got her eyes focusing again. Vandor sat to her left, a grin of sardonic amusement on his lips. To her right, Poole, the third of the trio who had backed Olaf on their first meeting, had a swollen top lip and a bruise under his left eye. Going by the way Poole glared at her, Calamity concluded that she had in some way been responsible for his injuries.

"What the hell fool game're you playing at?" Calamity demanded, looking at Vandor and seeing he carried her gunbelt across his saddle.

"Miss Eastfield wants you," Vandor answered and looked her over from head to toe. "You sure don't have any papers on you."

"Could allus make good 'n' certain," Poole suggested.

"We'll push on!" Vandor ordered. "Flo's got something in mind for her. Say, gal, we heard that Texas gun-slick of your'n rid out of town. Where'd he go?"

No matter how they had managed to enter the barn, or even if somebody in town had been helping them, the men did not have a reliable source of information. So it would do no harm if they thought that the Kid was no longer a factor in the game.

"Back south, the stinking-son-of-a-bitch!" Calamity spat out. "Took my money and's soon's the going got rough, he run out on me."

"You should've tried paying him a bonus," Poole said maliciously. "Same sort the boss gives Van he——"

The words ended as Vandor jumped his horse forward to face the other man. Anger twisted the handsome face and Vandor's right hand raised above the Smith & Wesson's butt.

"What did you say, Poole?"

"Hey! Easy there, Van! I was only fooling."

"Then don't!" Vandor warned, turning his horse and setting it moving. When Poole, leading Calamity, came alongside, he went on, "You watch your mouth, Poole. Else you're likely to get some more of what Flo gave you for missing the sheriff."

"I didn't miss him!" Poole protested. "That feller back in Hollick told us Leckenby was bad hit. His hoss carried him clear——"

"You was supposed to kill him," Vandor pointed out. "He came back to town alive and Olaf got killed."

"That was you 'n' Torp's doing, not mine!" Poole protested. "Anyways, why're you so all-fired worried about that crazy bastard? He was better off dead."

"I know it. You know it," Vandor said dryly. "But don't you ever let Flo hear you say it. Olaf was her brother and the best logger around until he had a tree drop the wrong way."

"That's how he got the scar and like he was, huh?" Calamity put in. "Poor son-of-a-bitch."

"That's how," Vandor agreed, looking at the girl. "I don't know what Flo's got in mind for you. But, was I you, I'd be scared."

"Could be I don't scare easy," Calamity answered, hoping that the icy cold sensation which ran along her spine would not make its effects noticeable.

"Maybe you ain't got enough good sense to be scared," Vandor sniffed. "But I'll tell you one thing, gal. If you're not dead by nightfall, it'll be because you're praying that you should be."

Having delivered his cryptic prediction, Vandor urged his horse on at a faster pace. Throwing a glance to their rear, Poole forced his and Calamity's mounts to keep up with the other animal. They were already out of sight of the town, riding through wooded country along the valley through which the Middle Loup River flowed. Hills rose on either side at that point and the valley wound through them.

After three hours continuous hard riding, they approached a place where the valley narrowed to a sheer-sided gorge. Coming out of the narrow stretch, the Loup widened to form a ford.

Calamity noticed that the shallows had been much used over the past couple of months or so, both shores being churned into soft mud by continual coming and going of men and heavy wagons. A narrow path ran up the side of the gorge toward which the party was riding, but they did not follow it. Turning the horses, they rode up the scar ripped across the more gentle slope of the valley by the same means that had created the muddy banks.

Reaching the top of the incline, Calamity found herself in a fair-sized clearing on nearly level ground. The sawmill's buildings fanned in a rough circle ahead of her. There were several log cabins designed to house the workers and supply their needs, or to hold stores. Most of them appeared to be empty as the girl rode nearer. That could be accounted for by the twenty or so horses in the pole corrals, most of which looked more suitable for draft-work than riding. Beyond the other buildings, backing on to a creek at the upper side of the gorge, was the sawmill itself, a large plank-built structure with chimneys for its steam-engines rising from the roof. Smoke curled lazily from one of the chimneys, and the sound of a circular saw working reached the girl's ears.

"Looks like the boss's fixing to take herself a ride," Poole remarked, nodding to where a fast-looking bloodbay gelding stood saddled, its reins looped on the hitching rail of a cabin clear of the others and close to the side of the gorge.

"She's fetching the rest of the boys in from Burwell most likely," Vandor answered, then raised his voice. "Torp!"

Coming from what would be the cookshack, followed by three more gun-hung hard-cases, Torp eyed the girl malevolently before turning his gaze to Vandor.

"See you got her."

"That's what I was sent to do," Vandor replied. "Where's the boss?"

"Her 'n' Logger's up at the mill, testing the gear," Torp answered. "Reckons they'll be starting work real soon."

"Could be she's right," Vandor grinned and dropped from his mount. "Bunjy, take my hoss and toss my saddle on another. Rest of you, get your rifles and go watch the trail."

"Somebody coming?" asked one of the men.

"A bunch from town," Vandor explained. "If Trinian's with 'em, the boss'll pay five hundred dollars to the feller who downs him."

Removing Calamity's gunbelt and draping it across his shoulder, Vandor went to the girl. He released first one foot, then the other, while the men disappeared into the cabin. Knowing that she could not hope to escape at that moment, Calamity swung her right leg up and forward to drop to the ground. Five men came from the cabin, carrying rifles, and moved off toward the trail. Taking hold of an arm each, Vandor and Poole hustled the girl toward the sawmill. Muttering under his breath, the man called Bunjy led off all three horses toward the corral.

Halting inside the doors of the mill, the men and Calamity watched and listened to the scream of the whirling circular saw as it ripped down the center of a sizeable tree trunk.

"Miss Eastfield!" Vandor called.

Looking over her shoulder, Florence smiled at the sight of the girl between the men. Like Calamity, she wore moccasins and had on a man's shirt and an old black skirt. With her sleeves rolled up, she showed a powerful pair of arms. Signaling to the burly man at the controls, she walked toward the newcomers. The man pulled on a lever, halting the log carriage which held another large trunk ready to be put through the saw.

"We've got her, Miss Eastfield," Poole announced.

"You wouldn't've showed your face back here if you hadn't," Florence answered coldly. "Was she carrying any papers, Mr. Vandor?"

"No," Vandor replied.

"It doesn't matter," Florence decided. "After we've dealt with her, we'll go over to Burwell and bring back the rest of the men. Then we'll visit Hollick City and have you elected sheriff."

"Maybe you'll have trouble getting the folks to vote for him," Calamity remarked, praying silently to have her hands free and a clear run at the blonde.

"I don't think so," Florence replied. "A town's only as tough as its leading citizens. Without Leckenby and maybe ten others, Hollick City is full of sheep. When I ride in, it will be with enough guns to make sure they know who's running things." Her eyes went to Vandor. "Is the Texan dead?"

"He left town last night, soon's he found out the sheriff'd been shot," Vandor replied. "Gal says he run out on her."

"Looks like we both had lousy luck with the fellers we hired to help us," Calamity remarked to Florence. "Mind if I sit down?"

Without waiting for the blonde to agree, Calamity went and sat on the bench by the doors. There was only one hope for her, to keep her captors occupied and talking. She must play for time in the hope that she could hold off whatever Florence intended to do with her until the Kid arrived. That he would come, Calamity did not doubt. Given luck, he ought to be on his way by that time. Every minute, second even, that she gained increased her chances of survival.

Going by the scowl Vandor directed at Calamity, he did not care for her references to the inadequacies of the male help. Turning from the girl, he diverted Florence's attention by pointing to the log at the far end of the carriage.

"Looks like everything's working properly, Miss Eastfield."

"The mill's been ready to go for a week or

more," Florence answered. "So's all the other gear. But none of it's any use unless we can float the logs in."

"So that's why you want my ranch!" Calamity ejaculated.

"What do you mean?" asked the blonde.

"You want it in case you can't make this game up here work!"

It seemed that Calamity's mocking words struck at a sore spot. Spinning around, Florence glared furiously at the girl.

"How do you mean, can't make it work?" the blonde spat out. "Maybe I don't run around dressed like a man, but I know more about the timber business, every part of it, than any damned logger you'll ever meet."

"If you're so all-fired smart," Calamity scoffed, "why'd you need the ranch?"

"I don't want, or need your ranch."

"That's not what you was saying in town."

"The *ranch* doesn't mean a thing to me!" Florence insisted.

"Then what the hell do you want?" Calamity asked.

"Timber."

"I've been riding for three or more hours through it," the girl pointed out. "Haven't seen the deeds to my place yet, but I don't reckon it takes in much of the wood country. And there's not many trees on the ranch."

"I agree," Florence replied.

"Maybe we ought to get going, Miss Eastfield," Vandor put in. "It's a fair ride into Burwell."

"Go check that the men are watching the trail, Poole," Florence ordered. "I won't be long, Mr. Vandor."

Calamity watched Poole turn and slouch away. That left Florence and Vandor in her immediate vicinity, the sawmill hand being at the far end of the building. So the girl determined to make a try at escaping, but knew that she must plan things very carefully if she hoped to succeed.

"I still reckon you want that ranch 'cause you know you can't make a go of this timber game," Calamity stated.

"Like hell I do!" Florence answered angrily. "It's just that the Loup and a few other streams run through your range."

"So?"

"So I need that water. I have to throw a dam across the bottom end of the gorge there to make the water back up and raise the level of the creeks and streams that run into it, so that we can float the timber here. And I can't do that unless I own the Rafter C."

"Why not?" Calamity inquired. "With all them guns you've got hired, you ought to be able to handle a four-man ranch crew."

Watching Florence's face, Calamity could see

worry lines on it. If the blonde was not grieving, she felt deeply concerned by Olaf's death. Whatever caused the emotion went deeper than the demise of the bald giant. Florence's cheeks reddened at the girl's increasingly mocking tone. Sucking in a deep breath, the blonde allowed it to come out again in an annoyed hiss.

"It was the law, not the ranch crew that stopped me damming the river."

"Day Leckenby?"

"No. This's ranching country and one of the State Legislature's laws is that you cannot deprive a ranch of its water supply."

"Which you'd've done if you threw that dam .across the Loup."

"Exactly," Florence agreed. "It wouldn't affect the ranchers further down the Loup; they have side streams that would give them enough for their needs."

"So that's what's behind it," Calamity growled. "You're willing to run the Trinians off their land just so that you can cut the timber up here."

"It didn't start out that way," Florence answered bitterly. "When I took the contract, nobody mentioned ab——"

"About the water rights of the ranchers," Calamity finished for her. "In other words, Flo, you got too——"

Stepping forward, Florence swung her right

hand in a slap that rocked the girl's head and almost tumbled her from the bench. Vandor glided forward, catching hold of Calamity's shoulder and forcing her to remain seated as she tried to rise and retaliate. Hotheaded as Calamity might be, she knew the value of caution. Trying to repay the blow right then would get her nowhere. So she held her temper under control and waited for Florence to continue.

"Nobody took me!" the blonde gritted, her whole attitude showing that she secretly agreed with Calamity. "I offered to buy the Trinians out honestly enough. But they wouldn't sell."

"Couldn't sell," Calamity corrected.

"Wouldn't, couldn't, it all meant the same to me; that I wasn't able to fulfill my contract. Then I learned they were trying to locate you to buy the ranch."

"And you fixed it through The Outfit so your hired guns got to me afore I saw Lawyer Talbot and learned about the ranch. Why not have me killed in Topeka?"

"The Outfit didn't want trouble there, or the chance of you being connected to one of their men," Florence admitted and Vandor let out a worried growl.

"Then you was real lucky that I had to be sent on to Counselor Talbot in Mulrooney," Calamity remarked, guessing that Vandor did not approve of his employer discussing The Outfit's affairs.

"Like hell it was luck!" Florence protested. "I wrote to Pinkerton's in Endicott's name and told them to have their man take you to Lawyer Grosvenor instead of to Talbot. That was planning, not luck."

"Either way," Calamity grinned, "it sure went sour on you."

"How'd you get hold of Ruiz's *sabino* and Hogue's bay?" Vandor demanded.

"Me 'n' the Kid killed 'em," Calamity answered without thinking.

"You and *who*?" Vandor spat out.

His attitude gave Calamity a warning and she decided against making known the true identity of her companion. If Vandor learned that the black-dressed Texan was the Ysabel Kid, he would figure that the story of the desertion was a lie.

"What's the idea of fetching me up here, Flo?" Calamity asked, ignoring the man. "Did you figure I'd be scared enough to sell out to you if you got hold of me?"

"Would you be?"

"Would you believe me was I to say 'yes'? "

"No," Florence replied. "You might agree to sell, but I doubt if you'd keep to doing it. So there's only one thing left."

"What'd that be?" asked Calamity.

"You're going to meet with an accident," Florence explained. "A very bad accident. It'll be fatal."

"Who'd you say helped you to down Hogue and Ruiz?" Vandor growled, moving closer to the girl.

Ducking her head, Calamity butted Vandor in the body with sufficient force to stagger him backward. Then the girl straightened up, meaning to use her feet or any other method to remove Florence from her path. Even as she came erect, Calamity felt a hand catch hold of her shoulder. Pulled around, she saw that Florence had not been taken as unawares as had the gunslinger. Having turned Calamity, the blonde threw a punch with her other fist. Putting her whole weight behind it, Florence drove up her hand. The knuckles impacted under Calamity's jaw. Lifted on to her toes, Calamity pitched on to her back unconscious.

"Get up!" Florence snapped at Vandor as Logger ran toward her. "She was right about one thing. We both had lousy luck in picking our male help."

Lurching erect, Vandor rubbed his chest and moved toward where Calamity sprawled motionless on the ground.

"I'll kill her!" the gunslinger spat out.

"My way," Florence interrupted. "Get hold of one of those crowbars, Logger. Lift that log on the carriage high enough for Mr. Vandor to slip a length of rope under it. Then put the girl on the log, fasten her there."

Picking up one of the big, wide-ended iron crowbars which were used for altering the positions of the logs on the carriage, Logger obeyed. Vandor paused for a moment, looking at the blonde.

"You mean you're going to——?"

"I'm going to arrange for an 'accident' to happen to Miss Martha Jane Canary," Florence answered coldly. "She has to die, or The Outfit will want to know why not."

"Yeah," Vandor agreed.

Already the girl knew enough to make trouble for a member of The Outfit and that organization was not noted for restricting its reprisals to the direct cause. If Martha Jane Canary lived, The Outfit were going to ask why and Vandor would be one of the people required to give an answer.

"And, in case anything goes wrong," Florence continued. "I want to be able to show anybody who can *demand* an answer that it was an accident. Way her body'll look after it's been through the saw, I doubt if there'll be too close an examination of how she died."

Collecting a length of rope that hung on the wall, Vandor went to do his part in the execution. Florence took hold of Calamity's ankles and dragged her toward the men. Leaving them to raise her, the blonde collected a small hammer and some nails from the stores area of the mill.

Opening her eyes, Calamity groaned. First she tried to move a hand to her jaw, then to sit up. Through the swirls of dizziness, she realized that she was held down on a hard, rough surface. An attempt to move her legs warned that her trousers were fastened against the sides—of a log.

Understanding of her position sank in like an icy cold knife. Turning her head from side to side, Calamity knew that her supposition had been correct. Managing to raise her shoulders, she looked down her body to where the shining serrated blade of the circular saw glinted at the other end of the carriage. Only by exerting all her willpower could she hold down a shudder as she swung her eyes back to Florence and the two men.

"Is this because I helped get your brother killed?" the girl asked Florence.

"Partly," the blonde admitted. "Partly because you humiliated me in town. But mainly so that you meet with a fatal 'accident.' Naturally I'll be horrified and distressed when I hear the news. But nobody can blame me if you get killed 'accidentally' while you're snooping around my sawmill."

"Reckon these two fellers'll go along with you on doing it?"

"They will. Logger's been blacklisted by every major timber company. He'll never get another job. So he'll do what I tell him to keep this one. And Mr. Vandor knows that he daren't let you live. The Outfit wouldn't like that at all. Start the saw, Logger. We're going to fetch in the rest of the men from Burwell."

"Sure, Miss Eastfield," Logger answered.

"Hey, fatso!" Calamity called as Florence turned away. "You'd better hope this works, 'cause if it don't and I get loose, I'm going to make you wish you'd never been born."

Chapter 15

WHERE'VE THEY GOT THE GAL?

~~~

"TEND TO THE BLASTED HORSES, BUNJY!" MUTTERED
the man assigned to that task by Vandor as he removed the last saddle. "Get me another ready!
I'd've been better off working as a wrangler on a
ranch."

With that he let the third horse free in the corral.
He had collected a rope from the bunkhouse and
took his time in selecting then catching a mount
for Vandor to use. While doing so, he looked at the
sawmill and wondered what was happening inside.
Still muttering, he leisurely saddled the horse and
led it from the corral. About to replace the poles of
the gate, a movement down the slope beyond the
enclosure attracted his attention. Hand dropping

to the butt of his Colt, he looked that way. With a grunt, he removed his hand. A dun gelding, riderless and without a saddle, was moving through the trees and bushes.

"Damn it!" Bunjy spat. "One of 'em must've got out. I'd best go get it or they'll say I let it slip by me."

With that, he fastened Vandor's mount to the corral, closed the gate and picked up his rope. Walking toward the horse, he tried to think who owned it and how it had escaped. It must belong to the sawmill, no other horses strayed that far into the wooded slopes.

Drawing closer, Bunjy noticed that the dun appeared to have been hard-ridden and was lathered heavily. Not a particularly bright man, he failed to detect any special significance from the animal's condition. It stood grazing beyond a thick, heavily foliaged dogwood bush. Advancing slowly and cautiously, so that he could get within rope-throwing distance, he had eyes for nothing but the horse.

Suddenly a hand and black-sleeved arm extended from beneath the bush and closed about Bunjy's forward ankle as it touched the ground, giving a sharp tug at it. Tumbling forward, the man opened his mouth to yell. His arrival on the ground drove the breath from his lungs. To his ears came a rustling of the foliage, then a knee rammed into his spine and pinned him down. He felt his re-

volver jerked from the holster and tried to struggle.
Apparently his unseen assailant had tossed the gun
aside, for the same right hand which had removed
it shoved off his hat and dug into his hair. Letting
out a grunt, Bunjy prepared to cut loose with a
louder sound as his head was dragged back and
up. Before the shout could be uttered, he saw
something which caused him to hurriedly revise his
opinion. Passing slowly through his range of vision, the enormous, razor-sharp blade of a bowie
knife sank and its cutting edge touched lightly
against his tight-stretched throat.

"Make one sound and it'll be your last!"
growled a savage voice. "When I move my knee,
roll over slow 'n' easy."

Feeling the knee and knife move, Bunjy obeyed.
He knew that his assailant had not gone far, a
view that was confirmed as he turned on to his
back. A tall, bare-headed, black-dressed man
dropped into a kneeling position astride Bunjy
and the bowie knife's point prodded under his
chin. Held flat on the ground by the figure's
weight and threat of the knife, Bunjy stared up at
an Indian-dark, savage face. Hearing footsteps approaching, Bunjy turned his head slowly. Any
hopes of a rescue that he felt died as he saw Cash
Trinian and a cowhand coming up the slope in his
direction.

"Wha—How——?" Bunjy croaked.

"From where I'm sitting," drawled the Ysabel Kid, "I'd say it was for me to be asking the questions."

"And, mister," Staff went on, holding the Kid's rifle almost reverently, "was I you, I'd right quick 'n' truthful come up with the answers. We've been riding too hard 'n' fast to want lies."

Clearly the young cowhand spoke from the bottom of his heart. In fact, Staff would never forget what he had just been through. Although able to ride almost from the time he could walk, the young cowhand had been hard pressed to keep up with his boss during the journey from Hollick City. Trinian, no mean hand on a horse, had at times been on the point of suggesting to the Kid that they make a slower pace.

On being told the news of Calamity's capture, the Kid, Trinian and Staff had reduced their horses' burdens to a minimum. Carrying only a reserve of ammunition, they had set out for the sawmill. Born and raised in Hollick County, Trinian had led his companions by a shorter, more direct route than that taken by Vandor's party. The way they had come did not offer easy traveling and they had crossed areas that would have been impossible to any but the finest horsemen. Avoiding the river trail, they had missed the men sent to cover it by Vandor.

When Trinian had announced that the sawmill lay up the next ridge, the Kid had suggested that they should scout the area on foot. The fact that Vandor had taken Calamity alive hinted that she would still be that way. For her rescuers to be discovered might prove fatal to the girl.

So the Kid had gone ahead, silently as a raiding Comanche. Seeing Bunjy leading the horses to the corral, the Kid realized that there was a chance of gaining information. Stalking the man would be difficult as there was a stretch of open ground to cover. So the Kid had decided that, if he could not reach Bunjy, the gunslinger must come to him.

With that in mind, Staff had been instructed to remove the saddle and bridle from his horse. Taking the animal, the Kid had led it up the slope until sure that the man in the corral would see it. Then he had hidden himself under the dogwood bush to await developments. Bunjy had responded as required and the Kid now possessed the means of obtaining information.

"Where're they holding the gal?" the Kid demanded.

"What g——?" Bunjy croaked.

Instantly the position of the knife changed, its point going to the center of the man's face.

"It's your nose," the Kid remarked with an icy casualness that warned he was not bluffing.

"Sh—They took her into the sawmill!" Bunjy yelped. "I dunno why or——"

"Sit up," ordered the Kid, coming to his feet.

Obediently, Bunjy forced himself into a sitting

position. Behind him, Staff raised the Kid's rifle and drove it downward. The butt cracked against the top of Bunjy's skull and he flopped backward limply.

"Hawg-tie him," ordered the Kid. "Why in hell didn't you whomp him with your own gun?"

"And chance busting it?" Staff replied, handing over the Winchester and kneeling to carry out the Kid's instructions.

At first, during the ride from the ranch to Hollick City, Staff had tended to be cold and distant toward the Kid. The young cowhand could not see why his boss had needed to ask a Texan to help them hand the sawmill bunch their needings. Before they had reached the town, Staff's opinion had begun to change. The way the Kid had handled the white stallion started the change and nothing Staff had seen since caused him to alter his view that, Texan or not, the Kid would do to ride the river with. Impressed by the Kid's ability as he had been while watching the capture of Bunjy, Staff answered the Kid's complaint in a typical cowhand manner.

Working quickly, Staff and Trinian lashed Bunjy's hands and feet with pigging thongs they had brought for that purpose. Gagging him with his own bandana, they rolled the limp, unresisting man under the bush that had sheltered and concealed the Kid. Then they rose and followed the Indian-dark Texan toward the buildings. Revolvers in hand, Trinian and Staff watched the rear of the cabins. Nobody challenged them, but the Kid gave a signal that brought them to a halt as they advanced alongside the cookshack.

Peering over the Kid's shoulder, Staff saw Florence Eastfield and Vandor going into a cabin in front of which was hitched a saddled horse. The Kid let them enter before resuming his advance toward the open double doors of the sawmill. The three men heard the sound of the steam engine and whirring of the saw, without connecting them to Calamity.

"Reckon that feller was telling the truth?" the Kid asked.

"He was too scared not to," Staff declared.

"Best take a look inside and make sure," Trinian suggested.

Nodding his agreement, the Kid led the way into the building. Unemotional as he usually appeared, he slammed to a halt and stared. Behind him, Trinian and Staff stood transfixed with horror at the sight of Calamity stretched out on the log, with a rope about her arms and torso, and trouser legs nailed to the wood. Moving forward on the carriage, the log was bearing the girl toward the blurring, whirring blade of the big circular saw.

"Lon!" Calamity croaked.

Even as the word broke from the girl, Trinian growled, "We've got to stop this damned thing!"

Looking for the means of doing so, and hoping

that they would recognize it when it came into their range of vision, the trio saw Logger standing by the control lever. With a snarl, the big man snatched up a lumberjack's peavey. Gripping the six-foot-long, stout wooden pole with its sharp-pointed spike and hook at the thicker end, Logger prepared to defend his last chance of holding down a well-paid job. Drink, the cause of his being blacklisted by the major logging companies, had dulled his mind to the point where he could think of only one thing at a time. So, concerned only with retaining a job that brought money for more liquor, he ignored the fact that the newcomers were carrying firearms. Not that he needed to worry on that count.

"No shooting!" warned the Kid, thrusting his Winchester into Staff's left hand as the young cowhand started to raise his revolver. "I'll take him!"

Given a moment and the cause to think, Staff saw the reason for the Kid's suggestion. At the sound of the shot, the rest of the sawmill's crew would return. Apart from Logger, according to Leathers' reports, they were all hired gun-slicks. That meant they possessed sufficient skill to make life mighty hectic for the rescuers.

So Staff held his fire and watched the Kid. Out slid the bowie knife and the Texan rushed toward the burly lumberjack. Snarling a curse, Logger sprang to meet his attacker. To Trinian and Staff, it seemed that concern for Calamity's safety had driven thought and good sense from the Kid. He was charging at the big man, apparently oblivious of the danger presented by the peavey's pike or hook. Drink had not slowed Logger's ability with the peavey. Gripping it in his two hands, he swung it sideways and aimed the hook in the direction of the Kid's ribs.

Tearing his attention from the Kid, Trinian gave thought to saving Calamity if the Texan failed to reach the lever and halt the carriage. One of the heavy crowbars leaned against the frame supporting the circular saw. Twirling away his Colt, Trinian leaped and caught it up. Already the log's end was within a foot of the V-toothed blade. Calamity had raised her head and shoulders as far as possible and her face was pale under its tan. Picking up the crowbar, Trinian thrust it into the narrowing gap. Lying across the carriage, the iron bar rode toward the saw.

With the peavey's hook driving at him, the Kid kicked both of his feet to the front and fell backward. Breaking his fall with his left hand, he felt the wind of the implement's passing. Carried forward by his momentum, Logger's feet straddled the Kid's legs. Bringing up his right boot, the Kid hooked it between Logger's thighs and behind the man's rump. Bending his right leg, the Kid heaved at Logger and prevented him from coming to a halt. Then the bowie knife thrust upward. Its point sank into Logger's body and the blade ripped across to lay open his entire stomach. Blood gushed from the wound, splashing down on the Kid as the stricken man continued to blunder onward. Letting the peavey drop, Logger clutched at his injury and sank first to his knees, then collapsed upon his face.

Rocking backward, the Kid bounded to his feet as soon as Logger had passed above him. Without as much as a glance at the man, the Kid dived forward and gripped the lever. He pushed at it without result, so reversed direction. At his pull, the lever began to move and behind him he heard the sound of the saw biting into the end of the log.

Creeping onward, pushing the crowbar ahead, the log's end was bitten into by the teeth. Then they struck against the far harder, less yielding material of the crowbar. A hideous screaming ripped the air as the rapidly-spinning blade met the crowbar and shattered teeth sprayed out. Luckily for them, the end of the log shielded Calamity, Trinian and Staff from the flying metal fragments. At first the carriage tried to force the log onward, but the Kid's operation of the control lever brought it to a stop.

Hurdling Logger's body, the Kid ran to Calamity. Still pale, showing some of the fear that she had felt, the girl looked sideways at her rescuer. Then she regained control of her emotions and managed to sound her usual self as she spoke.

"What the hell kept you?" she asked.

"Figured you was so comfy I didn't need to rush," the Kid answered, starting to sever the rope.

"Get me loose, blast it!" Calamity demanded, sitting up as soon as her torso had been freed.

"I'll do just that," promised the Kid, looking at the nails which held the girl's trouser legs to the log. "Only——"

"Cut the blasted things off!" Calamity insisted hotly. "I've got things to do to Flo Eastfi—— Behind you, Cash!"

While speaking to the Kid, Calamity had been looking around and a movement at the main doors caught her eye. She saw a shadow fall across it and yelled her warning instinctively. Spinning around, right hand flashing toward his Colt, Trinian found himself face-to-face with Poole. Recognition appeared to be mutual. On his way to tell Florence and Vandor that he had seen a couple of strange horses among the trees, Poole was not expecting trouble. He still reacted with some speed, but not fast enough. Clearing leather, Trinian's Army Colt crashed. The bullet ripped into Poole's chest. Spun around, he tumbled out through the door. As he went, his own revolver left its holster and bellowed. Its bullet churned into the ground as he fell.

"That does it!" Trinian growled, going to the door and flattening himself alongside it to look out. "There'll be more of 'em coming."

"Wasn't no other way you could've handled it," the Kid answered.

"Gimme that blasted knife!" Calamity yelled. "Damned if I didn't figure I'd have to get myself loose."

Handing the knife to the girl, the Kid caught his rifle, tossed to him by Staff. While the two men joined Trinian at the door, Calamity started to cut the material of first left, then right trouser leg. She had not completed her work when bullets impacted against the walls of the sawmill and the Kid's Winchester cracked in reply. Unbuckling her waistband, she wriggled from the ruined trousers. Lead sent splinters flying from the log and Calamity quit it with her shirt tail flapping around her drawers.

Calamity saw her gunbelt on the bench, so made for it. To reach it, she had to pass across the open doors. Disregarding the danger, she hurled herself forward. A bullet fanned by her head and she heard the flat bark of the Kid's rifle. Looking through the door, she saw a man staggering toward one of the cabins. Dropping his rifle, he fell before he reached safety. Two more strides carried Calamity beyond the door. Reaching down her right hand, she snatched free her whip. Ignoring the Colt, she darted toward the side door through which Florence and Vandor had left the building.

With the returning hard-cases beyond any range

at which he could hope to make a hit with his revolver, Staff took time out to glance around. He saw Calamity about to go through the side door.

"Where're you going, Calam?" Staff called.

"To keep a promise!" the girl answered and departed.

"What's up, Staff?" called the Kid, turning his attention from where Torp and the other men were taking cover among the empty cabins.

"Calam's going after Flor——" the young cowhand answered without looking around. "Look out, gal."

Raising his voice to yell the last three words, he lunged through the door and his revolver cracked twice. From some distance beyond the door, two shots mingled with the detonations from Staff's gun. Letting out a cry of pain, the youngster returned through the door. The revolver dropped from his hand and he collapsed face down on the floor.

Dashing across the sawmill, Trinian dropped to one knee by the cowhand. The Kid accompanied the rancher, looking at the hideous hole where the two heavy caliber bullets had burst out of the left side of Staff's back, then stepped cautiously to the door.

"He's cashed, Kid," Trinian growled bitterly.

"Looks like he got his saving Calam," the Kid replied. "Did a good job of it at that."

Coming to his feet, Trinian joined the Kid and

looked out of the building. Vandor sprawled face down, revolver a couple of feet away from his hand, at the rear of the cabin they had seen him enter with Florence. From Vandor, Trinian turned his attention to where Calamity was disappearing around the corner at the front of the building.

Chapter 16

I WARNED YOU WHAT'D HAPPEN

LEAVING THE SAWMILL, CALAMITY DARTED TOWARD the cabin where she expected to find Florence East-field. Her hope of taking the blonde and Vandor by surprise did not materialize. Down at the corral, Vandor turned from his horse. Drawing his Smith & Wesson, he started to run in the girl's direction. Yelling his warning, Staff burst from the door of the big building. Calamity heard the crackle of shots followed by the cowhand's cry of pain, then watched Vandor go down. By that time she had reached a position which offered a view of the front of the cabin. What she saw prevented her from turning to discover how badly her rescuer had been injured.

At the hitching rail, Florence had already unfastened her horse's reins and was preparing to mount. She gripped the saddle-horn in her right hand, drawing up the hem of her black skirt with the other hand as she raised her left foot toward the stirrup iron. The sound of shots from the sawmill had caused Florence to revise her plans. Instead of changing into her riding clothes and ensuring that the red-haired girl was dead before leaving, she had decided to make an immediate departure. After collecting the reinforcements waiting at Burwell, she could return and deal with whatever situation awaited her. Looking across the horse at Calamity, Florence figured that she had made a wise choice. With the girl free, Florence would need the extra gunhands if she hoped to enforce her will on the people of Hollick County.

Guessing what the blonde had in mind, Calamity also realized that Florence would be mounted and gone unless she acted fast. So the girl took aim and swung her right arm. The whip's long lash extended before Calamity and its popper struck with an explosive crack against the horse's rump. Letting out a scream of pain, the animal reared and plunged forward. Florence felt the saddle-horn snatched from beneath her right hand and the force of the jerk sent her staggering. Staying on her feet, she caught her balance and prepared to chase after the fleeing horse.

Up and down moved Calamity's right hand.

Once again her aim proved very accurate and she demonstrated her skill at using the whip. Curling in the required direction, the rawhide popper sliced into the top right side of Florence's skirt. It cut through the material, tangling with the keys in her pocket. With a heave on the handle, Calamity caused the lash to rip the skirt. The blonde's screech of anger rang loud as the force of Calamity's pull spun her around and peeled off the skirt to expose her plump, shapely legs and frilly-edged drawers. Trying to resume her pursuit of the horse, Florence heard the hiss of the whip's lash passing through the air. Cold on her bare skin, the plaited leather coiled around her ankles and jerked them together so that she tumbled to the ground.

Florence might have counted herself fortunate. In skilled hands, the bull-whip was a weapon combining the cutting power of a knife and crushing pressure of a closing bear-trap. If Calamity had wished, she could have peeled flesh instead of stripping off the skirt, or broken both of Florence's ankles.

Hitting the ground, Florence broke her fall with her hands. Calamity deftly shook the lash free, ignoring the shouts of the men behind her. Grim satisfaction showed on the girl's face as she watched Florence twist toward her. Resting her left knee on the ground, Florence forced herself up on her hands.

"I warned you what'd happen if I got loose,"

Calamity remarked, tossing her whip over Florence to where the land dipped gently to the lip of the gorge.

Instantly Florence catapulted herself forward, trying to ram her skull into the girl's chest. Expecting some such move, Calamity twisted her torso and the blonde's head scraped by her side. Florence's left shoulder struck Calamity and the woman's arms wrapped about the girl's waist. Despite having anticipated the attack, Calamity felt herself forced backward by Florence's weight. Linking her hands under the blonde's plump midsection, she fell backward. Unable to stop herself, Florence was drawn after the girl. On landing, Calamity's knees jabbed into the blonde's upper thighs. Florence felt herself hoisted into the air. Losing her hold on the girl's waist, she felt herself released and turned a somersault to land on her back.

Rolling over swiftly and rising on one knee, Calamity lunged at Florence. Kneeling astride the woman's head, she dug her fingers into the other's left breast. A squeal broke from Florence, but she showed that she knew a trick or two. Bringing up her legs, she snapped them together so that the insides of her knees struck Calamity's ears. Pain caused the girl to release her hold, rear up and stagger away.

Oblivious of the gunfire that crackled intermittently among the buildings, Florence rolled over and started to rise. As Calamity rushed at her, the blonde shot out a punch. It took the girl in the stomach, halting her and causing a retreat that let the woman stand up. They came together in a flurry of flying fists. There was no skill in either's attack, only a melee of flailing arms that propelled knuckles into the other's face, bust, torso, ribs, or missed with equal abandon. For almost a minute the exchange of blows continued. Fists smacked flesh to the accompaniment of gasps, squeals and croaked curses from their recipients. In the course of their slugging, they trampled over Calamity's whip and gave it no thought.

Abruptly Florence changed her tactics. Blood was running from her nostrils and she snorted them clear as she dug both hands into Calamity's hair. Taking a firm hold, the blonde stepped backward and pivoted around. Caught by surprise, Calamity was dragged off balance. Releasing the hair, Florence threw but missed with a hay-maker of a blow. Set free, but unable to stop herself, Calamity was propelled down the slope, stumbled and sprawled on her hands and knees. Looking in the direction from which she had come, the girl saw something that sent a chill running through her.

Instead of following Calamity, Florence had bent and snatched up the whip. From all appearances, the blonde knew how to handle it. Maybe not to the girl's standard, but sufficient for her needs. Advancing, Florence swung the whip and aimed its lash at the redhead. Calamity twisted over, hearing the savage crack and watching the popper churn a groove into the ground where her body had been an instant before. Taking another two strides, Florence tried again. This time Calamity felt the lash bite through her shirt as she rolled. Pain slowed her reactions, preventing her from grabbing at the lash. Yet she knew that she had been lucky. If the popper had caught her, instead of higher up the lash, it would have bitten deep into her flesh. While painful, the section that struck her merely raised a weal across her back.

Again the lash hissed and drove a burning sensation through the girl. She rolled over and found herself at the edge of the gorge. Looking back, she knew that she was in even greater danger. Florence had not come closer, so the distance separating them was just right for Calamity to receive the full impact of the popper when the next attack was delivered. Back rose the blonde's arm, the long lash following its movement with sinuous grace.

In the sawmill, the Kid and Trinian heard the first crack of Calamity's whip and saw Florence's horse departing without a rider. Their place at the door prevented them from witnessing what was going on at the front of the cabin, but the Kid could guess at Calamity's next actions.

"We'd best stop them gun-slicks horning in while ole Calam hands that Eastfield gal her needings," the Kid suggested.

"Let's do just that," Trinian agreed, glancing at Staff's body.

Holding his rifle in what soldiers called the "high port" position of readiness, the Kid stepped from the building. Trinian followed him and they were about to go along to the front when Torp and another of Florence's hands came around the corner. Holding revolvers, the sawmill pair slammed to a halt and stared at their intended victims. They had believed that Trinian and the Kid were by the front entrance and finding otherwise handed them a hell of a shock.

Down swiveled the Kid's rifle, lining at Torp from hip level. Four times, so fast that the detonations sounded like the rolling of a drum, the Winchester spat out lead that ripped through Torp's body. Although the man got off a shot as he was thrown backward, the bullet drove into the wall above the Kid's head. Sidestepping, Trinian moved clear of the Kid and cut loose with his Army Colt. He sent a .44 ball into the second hard-case's head before the other recovered from the surprise.

"Get back inside!" barked the Kid, seeing the barrel of a rifle poke around the corner of one of the store cabins.

Spinning on his heel, Trinian leaped into the sawmill. He missed death by inches as a man fired at him from the main entrance. Although his Colt barked in reply, the bullet missed and the man retreated uninjured. Coming in on Trinian's heels, the Kid suggested that they should keep the double doors covered.

"Sure," the rancher agreed, starting across the building. "I don't know how many of 'em's left, but they're all gunhands."

"Here," the Kid said, taking his right hand from the Winchester to draw his Dragoon and offer it to Trinian. "You might need some extra bullets quicker'n you can reload."

"Thanks," Trinian replied, accepting the revolver in his left hand.

On reaching the front entrance, they saw the man who had exchanged shots with Trinian diving through the door of the nearest cabin. Darting across the open space to reach the farther side of the entrance, Trinian heard two bullets split the air above him.

"One of 'em's in the cookshack and t'other's laid alongside that third cabin," the Kid announced, then grinned as he looked to where the two women were slugging it out near the gorge. "With them tangled up close, Eastfield's bunch won't chance trying to hit Calam."

Apparently the three gunslingers agreed with the Kid. Ignoring their boss' predicament, they began to bombard the entrance of the sawmill. The hail of bullets caused the Texan and Trinian to duck inside and they did not see Calamity thrown down the incline or Florence's use of the whip.

"The gal's've gone," the Kid said after an ineffectual if lengthy trading of shots. "Let's load up, then I'll go through the side door and to the East-field cabin. That way we'll have 'em in a cross-fire."

"It'd be best," Trinian agreed. "If we can nail another one, his pards won't be so eager to keep fighting."

While Trinian went through the slow process of recharging his Army Colt's chambers with paper combustible cartridges and replaced the used percussion caps, the Kid fed metal-case bullets through the loading slot of his Winchester. Holding a fully loaded rifle, the Kid wondered how Calamity was faring.

Even as the whip's lash snaked in her direction, Calamity knew what she must do. Swinging her legs around, she lowered herself over the edge of the gorge. Dirt flew into her face as the popper hit the ground between her hands. Spluttering, she let go and dropped about twelve feet on to the path that ascended the face. On landing, she pressed herself against the rock. At that point there was a slight overhang to hide her from Florence. Fighting to hold down the sound of her breathing, Calamity stood with her face and body flattened to the wall.

"It's no good hiding, Canary!" Florence's voice warned from above. "I can still get to you."

With that the blonde swung the whip, its lash curling down over the contours of the wall. Calamity gritted her teeth to prevent as much as a gasp leaving her as the leather bit into her back. Again the whip cracked and she saw the lash strike the wall to her left. Like a flash she turned and grabbed it in both hands. Bracing herself, she tugged hard. Taken unawares, Florence gave a startled yell. She knew that she could not prevent herself going over, so jumped. Releasing the whip's handle, she landed on the edge of the path. For a moment she teetered and then slipped. Grabbing wildly, she managed to hook her arms over the edge and dangle from it.

Once again Calamity discarded her whip, then walked toward Florence. Kneeling, the girl obtained a double-handed hold on the blonde hair and hauled the woman upward. Florence squealed and mouthed curses at the pain that it caused. Hooking her right leg on to the path, Florence made sure that she would not fall. Then she drove her right fist into Calamity's left breast. Releasing the hair with a croak of agony, Calamity staggered backward.

During the brief seconds Calamity required to shake off the worst effects of the blow, Florence regained the path and stood up. Neither of them gave a thought to the whip, but came together in a fist-swinging rush. After exchanging wild blows, they closed in a tight clinch and locked their arms around each other in a double bear hug. Trying to trip Florence, Calamity slid her right leg between the blonde's meaty thighs and behind her left knee.

At the same moment, the woman duplicated the move. Balancing precariously as they crushed breast to breast at each other, they tilted over. Still enmeshed in each other's grasp, they crashed to the path on their sides. The impact broke their holds and Florence rolled Calamity over, kneeling astride her and driving her hands at her face. Calamity jerked her head forward, closing her teeth on the base of Florence's right forefinger. With a screech, the blonde pulled back and Calamity pitched her over.

Landing on top, Calamity tied into Florence in a savage, unthinking tangle. For over two minutes they turned, pitched and rolled on the path. Sometimes they were face-to-face, then one behind the other, or head to foot—all the while ripping, biting, tearing, punching, kneeing, kicking and clawing. During the mindless brawl, Calamity's shirt was torn off and Florence lost her blouse.

Just how it happened, neither woman could tell; but they made their feet with Florence behind Calamity and holding her in a full Nelson. Arms hooked under Calamity's and fingers interlaced behind her neck, Florence saw her chance. Gasping in breaths of air with a sound like a saw rasping into wood, the blonde began to push Calamity toward the wall of the gorge.

When all their weapons were fully loaded, the Kid nodded to Trinian and crossed to the side door. Reaching it, he made a discovery that changed his plan of campaign. Vandor was not dead and, as the Kid appeared, was already riding his horse out of sight behind Florence's cabin.

Nicked by one of Staff's bullets, Vandor had been stunned. On his recovery and return to conscious thought, he had reached a rapid decision on what to do next. Going by the shooting that he heard, some of his companions were alive and fighting. Not that he meant to go and help them. The Canary girl had escaped, so Vandor could expect no mercy from her rescuers should he fall into their hands. If he knew Florence, she would already be riding at all speed for the safety of Burwell. Catching up with her and reaching the town offered him his only hope of salvation. With that in mind, he had retrieved his Smith & Wesson, collected his horse and set it moving.

The Kid recognized a threat to Calamity. If Vandor laid hands on her, the girl would make a useful hostage. So the Kid stepped through the door, meaning to go after the man. A bullet from the end of the third cabin hissed by his face and caused his hurried return to the building.

"Vandor's getting away, Cash!" the Kid yelled. "I'm going after him."

"Go to it," the rancher answered. "I'll cover you."

Instead of trying to leave by the side door, the Kid went to the rear entrance. If he must run the gauntlet through the fire of the men in the cabins, he aimed to do it Comanche fashion. A shrill whistle left the Kid's lips. Hearing it, his white stallion loped swiftly up the slope. Running to meet his horse, the Texan took off in a bound that landed him afork the saddle without touching the stirrups or reins looped around the horn. Rifle in his right hand, he urged the stallion to a better speed and prayed that he would be in time to save Calamity.

Knowing that she might be seriously injured if she allowed Florence to crash her face and bust into the wall, Calamity let the woman hustle her forward. When close enough, she swung up and rested her feet on the side of the gorge. Letting her legs bend, Calamity straightened them with enough force to thrust her captor backward. Before the blonde could escape, they had crossed the path and fallen over the edge. Separating in midair, they plunged into the river.

They landed in a deep pool where the current formed a swirling eddy. Spluttering and gasping, Calamity came up first. The icy chill of the water had done nothing to cool off her temper. As Florence's head bobbed above the surface, she caught the girl's fist on the nose. Then Calamity grabbed the woman's hair and shoved her under. She felt Florence's fingers close on the neck of her undershirt and haul her down. Clinging together, they submerged and continued to fight under water. With her lungs seeming to be almost bursting, Calamity got her face briefly above the surface.

She had barely time to suck in a mouthful of air before Florence dragged her down. A plump arm waved into view, followed by a blonde head. Florence spat out water, making incoherent sounds, then one of Calamity's hands took hold of the tangled hair and she disappeared again. Ripped off by Florence's grabbing hands, Calamity's undershirt floated to the surface.

Fingers sank into flesh, grinding and crushing, as the current carried the fighting women from the eddy. Over and over they turned, breathing when they could. Half drowned but showing no sign of breaking off hostilities, they were swept on to the shallows beyond the gorge.

With her chemise torn and trailing from her waist, Florence managed to make her feet. Also naked to the waist, Calamity rose with her. Fear and desperation gave the blonde enough strength to thrust the girl away from her. Sobbing in exhaustion, beaten and scared, Florence stumbled through the shallows toward the shore. Her feet sank into the mud churned up by the wagons which brought in her supplies and building materials, slowing down her flight. Following Florence, Calamity dived to lock her arms around the other's waist. Down they went together, rolling and struggling in the clinging, gooey mud.

At last Calamity felt herself gaining the upper hand. Aching in every muscle and fiber, smothered from head to foot in mud, the girl straddled Florence's torso. With knees pinning down the blonde's arms, Calamity scooped up hands full of mud and heaped the stuff on her victim's face. Unable to see or breathe, Florence used her rapidly failing strength in feeble attempts to roll the girl from her.

Sanity returned to Calamity, along with a realization of what she was doing. Then she heard shooting and, closer, the drumming of hooves. Raising her head, she saw Vandor galloping down the slope. It seemed that recognition was mutual, for the man snatched out his revolver.

Staring at the two mud-covered figures, Vandor needed to ride almost to the foot of the slope before he could tell for sure who was on top. The Smith & Wesson had been drawn as no more than a precaution, but he knew at last that he would have to use it. Not only could he win Florence's increased gratitude by rescuing her, but the girl knew enough to bring the wrath of The Outfit on his head. Reining in his horse, he raised the revolver shoulder high, took aim and squeezed the double-action trigger.

Almost mad with terror, Florence felt Calamity relax. Taking advantage of the girl being distracted by Vandor, the blonde expended the dregs of her energy to heave herself into a sitting position. Too late Vandor saw what was happening. Even as the Smith & Wesson's hammer reached the point where it was set free to snap forward again,

Calamity tumbled away and Florence rose. The revolver crashed and its bullet flew across the mud to drive into the center of the woman's back.

Tipped sideways by Florence's surging thrust, Calamity landed on her hands and lay staring toward Vandor. Controlling his horse as Florence collapsed on to her back, he swung the gun into line with the certainty that this time nothing could come between himself and the girl.

Urging his horse to a full gallop, the Kid guided it by knee-pressure. The moment he emerged from behind Florence's quarters, he twisted in the saddle and pointed the rifle toward the third cabin. Lead made its eerie crack in the air before the Kid's face. Instantly his Winchester began to crash, throwing bullets in the direction of the man sheltering alongside the cabin. At the same moment, the second man burst out of the cookshack and the third reappeared through the door he had entered after being driven from the sawmill. Their rifles were lifting shoulderward ready for use.

Five times in rapid succession the Kid's Winchester spat flame. Splinters erupted from the four holes which developed in the cabin's wall and drew ever closer to the hard-case's position. On the fifth shot, the man jerked convulsively. The bullet caused no splinters to fly, but had hit him in the head.

Seeing the Kid's danger, Trinian dashed from the sawmill's front entrance. With a revolver in each hand, he ran toward the third of the Kid's attackers. Hearing the rancher, the man swung around fast. Rifle and Army Colt roared almost at the same instant. Trinian's Stetson spun from his head, but he saw his own bullet bury itself in the man's left shoulder. Throwing aside the rifle, the wounded man spun around and fell.

With his bullets coming closer to the Kid, the second gunslinger became aware of the fresh danger. Swiveling to face Trinian, he lined his sights on the rancher. Timing the move just right, Trinian went down in a rolling dive. He heard the rifle crack, but its bullet passed above him. Ending his evasion on his stomach, he cut loose with both revolvers. Their bullets struck the man in the body, flinging him off his feet.

When no more shots came his way, the Kid concluded that Trinian's intervention had been successful. Reaching the top of the slope, he saw Vandor send the bullet into Florence. Quitting the stallion's back at full gallop, the Kid landed with cat-like agility. Then he dropped into a kneeling position, working with smooth, unflurried speed for all the urgency of the situation.

Weakly Calamity tried to rise, but the pain and exhaustion that filled her were too much for movement. She watched the Smith & Wesson turn to point at her, moving at what seemed to be a snail's pace, its .44-caliber muzzle looking like the yawning mouth of a cannon.

Suddenly the vague shape behind the revolver stiffened and jerked. His face appeared to dissolve into bloody ruin and the right arm flopped limply to release the revolver. Feeling its rider sliding from the saddle, the horse snorted and moved off. Shot in the head by the Kid, Vandor sprawled face down into the mud.

Even as the Kid rose, working the Winchester's lever to replace the bullet which had saved the girl's life, he saw riders galloping along the Hollick City trail. Led by Doctor Goldberg, six well-armed men plunged their horses through the ford. Telling his companions to keep going, the doctor dismounted at Calamity's side. The girl's response to Goldberg asking if he could help her was typical of Calamity Jane.

"I—I'll do!" she gasped. "See—if—you can—help—Flo——"

And Calamity collapsed unconscious.

Chapter 17

IF YOU CAN MEET MY PRICE

"WELL, CALAM, IT'S ALL OVER," CASH TRINIAN announced. "We found papers in Miss Eastfield's safe. Took with what those two gun-slicks we caught 'n' Lawyer Endicott told us, we've learned the whole game."

It was sundown on the day after the fight at the sawmill. Calamity sat on a comfortable chair in the Leckenbys' parlor, while the sheriff's wife and Corey-Mae Trinian bustled about making everything ready for a celebration dinner. Standing by the fire, the Ysabel Kid grinned as he studied the girl's blackened right eye and swollen lip. From what Doctor Goldberg had mentioned about her injuries, ole Calam must be sore as hell; but she gave no sign of it.

Taking charge of Calamity while the other men attended to the dead and wounded sawmill gunslingers, Goldberg had washed the mud from her. Then he had treated her injuries and obtained clothing from Florence's cabin for the girl to wear during her return to Hollick City.

Finding Florence's keys in the torn skirt, Trinian and the Kid had opened the safe in the office. They had collected all the documents, gathered up Calamity's whip and gunbelt, bringing the items in for the sheriff's inspection. With Endicott's help, most aspects of the affair had been cleared up.

"Seems like Miss Eastfield figured to make enough on that contract to set her up in the timber business," the Kid remarked. "Only she needed her brother. She never let on about his accident and made sure the fellers who gave her the contract didn't meet him. They thought she was just acting for Olaf and he come in handy for making the loggers work, or would have. Trouble being, she'd took the contract afore she learned about the water-rights laws. Endicott told her about them and more."

"That gun-slick I shot reckons Miss Eastfield and Vandor got Endicott liquored up and he let on how we was trying to find you and buy the Rafter C, Calam," Trinian explained. "Told her about the arrangements with Counselor Talbot 'n' every damned thing. I'm acting as deputy until Day's back on his feet. If you want, I'll arrest Endicott."

"No!" Calamity stated flatly, glancing at Mrs. Leckenby. "Let it ride, Cash. He saw me yesterday and told me everything. Says he's through law-wrangling and that's good enough for me."

The sheriff's wife let out a sigh of relief, for she had wondered how Calamity intended to deal with her brother's breach of trust. Nodding his agreement, Trinian continued to discuss the affair with Calamity and the Kid. They decided that the girl should tell Marshal Beauregard everything on returning to Mulrooney, leaving him to decide what action, if any, could be taken against The Outfit. Calamity looked disturbed when she learned that Staff had left a widowed mother. Not until after an enjoyable meal, however, did Trinian raise the matter which most concerned him.

"What're you fixing to do with the Rafter C, Calam?" he asked, watching the girl limp stiffly across to sit in the well-padded armchair.

Instinctively Corey-Mae moved to her husband's side. Leaning by the fireplace, the Kid watched the couple's and Calamity's faces. Mrs. Leckenby put aside her intention of clearing the table and listened to the conversation that followed.

"It's a right nice-looking place," the girl answered. "I bet I could get nine, ten thousand dollars for it."

"You could," Trinian agreed coldly.

"So I'll sell it to you. If you can meet my price."

Trinian jerked his head around to look at his

wife, but Corey-Mae's eyes never left Calamity's unsmiling face.

"How much?" Trinian inquired warily.

"There's some'd say five thousand one hundred and fifty simoleons'd be a fair price," Calamity answered.

"Five thous——!" Trinian barked.

"That's what it cost pappy," Calamity pointed out, looking as sober and unfeeling as a hanging-judge about to pass a sentence of death. "He started out with one hundred and fifty dollars 'n' won the spread on a five-thousand-dollar call in a poker game. So there's some'd say that'd be a fair price."

"But you don't see it that way?" Corey-Mae said quietly.

"I don't," Calamity admitted.

"Then how do you see it?" Trinian demanded.

"Like I said, pappy started out with a hundred and fifty lil iron men," the girl replied and a grin started to twist at the corners of her mouth. "So you give me that and split the rest between the sheriff 'n' Staff's mother, seeing's it was through me they got shot up."

Silence followed the girl's words. Corey-Mae looked triumphantly at her husband and Trinian stared blankly, with mouth dropping open, at the red-haired girl in the armchair.

"Who's going to buy me that new shirt I got promised?" asked the Kid.

"Hell, yes!" Calamity ejaculated. "I forgot that. Cash, the price's gone up. I want a new shirt for Lon on top of it."

"But—But——" Trinian gobbled, hardly able to believe that he had heard correctly.

"It's my only offer," Calamity declared. "And, happen you've any feeling for the good folks of Hollick County, you'll take me up on it."

"I don't follow you," Trinian said.

"If you don't buy the place," Calamity explained, "I'll settle on it myself."

"Which means you'd have fire, flood, storms, drought, Injun raids and every other kind of misery 'n' torment come a-running here," the Kid elaborated.

"How you talk, Lon Ysabel," Miss Martha Jane Canary snorted indignantly. "Why you'll have folks believing I deserve to be called 'Calamity.' "